Leopold Murphy Defrocked
By David Spitz

1

It was impossible to tell whom the archbishop was more upset with, me or Fr. Marzano. He glared across his desk at the two of us, cheeks bright red under his violet zucchetto, nostrils flared aggressively. The first words out of his mouth were, "I don't believe it. I really don't. When I woke up this morning, this was not how I expected to be spending my goddamn Sunday afternoon. Now either this is a very, *very* inappropriate joke, or one of you, or *both* of you, has completely lost his mind."

"If I've lost my mind, it's all right with me," I thought, crossing my arms over my chest.

Marzano, meanwhile, squirmed in his chair most unbecomingly. Cowards are insufferable in general, as are the elderly. Combine them in the body of one man, and give that man some small speck of importance he might lose, and what you have then is an utterly detestable soul.

The archbishop turned to him and said, "You're sticking with your story? You never read the final draft?"

Marzano eagerly vomited up the affirmative.

I noticed that he began to perspire about halfway through his evasions, causing him to look not unlike the portrait of Jesus Christ, which adorned the far wall. *Agony in the Garden.* It wasn't the original Bellini, of course, just some gloomy knockoff, fitting décor given the sepulchral nature of the archbishop's office. It was hard to imagine any pastoral work ever getting done here. The room was dark, cold, and stale. Heavy curtains shut out whatever sunlight might've crept inside. The stink of incense lingered in the air.

"But what about the copy-editors?" the archbishop wanted to know. "Didn't anyone look at this thing before it went to press?"

"Unfortunately not, your Grace. We were up against the clock. It was all very frantic. You remember how it is at the *Review*. There's always an emergency somewhere, and so everything becomes chaos right at the last moment."

"Dammit, Marzano!"

The old priest flinched as if attached to one of those electro-shock machines. He cowered pathetically, eyes cast to the floor. A string of inaudible mumbling dribbled from his lips.

"What's that? Speak clearly. I can't understand a word you're saying."

"Your Grace, please, I've worked at *St. John's Review* for over thirty years. I've served as editor-in-chief for more than a decade. Nothing like this has every happened under my watch." He looked up, hoping to find mercy in the eyes of his archbishop, but the gaze that met him was pure hostility. Panicked now, Marzano glanced quickly about the room, searching for anything that might save him. His eyes fell upon me. "It was his fault. Murphy. He's the one who did this. It's true I asked him to write the piece, but I never expected him to submit something like this. How could I have known? The initial draft was nothing at all like the final version. Your Grace, you have to believe me. He didn't send it in until the very last minute, and on top of that, he assured us that the changes were insignificant."

Marzano stiffened now and spoke his next words in a more confident tone of voice, which only increased my loathing for him. A coward is one thing, but a coward who insists on a shadow-play of dignity! The old man was lucky he was sitting out of strangling range.

"I won't make excuses," he said. "Clearly this whole situation would never have happened without egregious oversights on the part of me and my staff, and if you deem it appropriate for me to resign my post, I shall of course obey without dissent. However, before you make too hasty a ruling, I only ask you to consider a few relevant facts. First, I have served the Church faithfully for many years. Second, Murphy, I don't pretend to know what's going on inside his head, but the man must either be deranged or else harbor some personal vendetta against me the cause of which I swear I do not know. Third—"

"That's enough," snapped the archbishop, more than a little annoyed. "You can save your breath. No one's asking you to resign. So long as you and Murphy weren't conspiring on this—"

"No, of course not," said the old priest with theatrical repugnance, after which, he allowed himself a smug glance in my direction. He was looking a hell of a lot more comfortable now that he'd dangled his bullshit resignation offer. Leaning back in his chair and adjusting the white collar around this throat, he concluded, "The simple fact is I had nothing to do with this."

Gutless but not inaccurate.

In the interval that followed, a deep silence settled over the room. The archbishop put a hand to his chin as he considered Marzano's defense. My eyes wandered back to the portrait of Jesus praying in the Garden of Gethsemane. I noticed red drops of paint dotting the rock over which Christ knelt. Hematidrosis this was called, a real-life medical phenomenon in which blood oozes from the skin like sweat. Apparently, such a thing could happen under instances of acute stress, such as when contemplating one's eminent crucifixion.

3

"Very well," said the archbishop at last. He looked at Marzano again and told the old man to leave us. They would talk later at more length.

"Yes, your Grace. Of course. Thank you, your Grace. God bless you. Goodbye, your Grace. God bless you. Goodbye."

He stumbled out of the office like a fool. I couldn't help but smirk.

"Something funny, Murphy? No, I insist. Explain to me the humor of this farce."

Truth be told, there was actually much to chuckle at here. To start, consider the average reader of *St. John's Review*. Age: Advanced. Politics: Conservative. Religion: Roman Catholic. Hobbies: Daily Mass, judging homosexuals. This morning, all over Chicago, folks like this had cracked open their papers and discovered an essay by Fr. Leopold Murphy entitled "Three Cheers for Pontius Pilate: A Theological Meditation on the Paschal Mystery." I wondered, sitting there in the archbishop's office, how long it took most people to choke on their steel-cut oatmeal and spit up their prune juice.

"Well? Are you going to defend yourself?"

I cleared my throat and made a show of putting on a serious face. "Intellectual rigor," I said. "That's what Marzano asked for. He didn't want just another touchy-feely reflection, so what I wrote is—"

"What you wrote isn't intellectually rigorous," spat the archbishop. "It's an attack. It's disgraceful and offensive, and you know it."

I allowed him a moment to cool off before replying.

"I humbly disagree, your Grace. You've said yourself it's a shame that so many Catholics have fallen away from the Church because they've lost sight of our rich philosophical tradition. This is true. Folks today, especially the young, when they think of religion, they think of gooey-brained virgins and wackos bombing abortion clinics. And why wouldn't they?"

4

In answer to this, the archbishop reached into his desk and produced a copy of that morning's *St. John's Review*. He opened it to my essay where I noticed that the most blasphemous portions of the text had been marked off in bright pink highlighter. There were angry-looking notes scrawled all the way down the margins.

He read, "When considered in light of all available evidence, it becomes clear that the Paschal Mystery is in fact no mystery at all. I ask you, who wouldn't crucify God if given the chance? He who created pain, death, misery, who sent the plagues down upon Egypt and tortured Job to win a bet, who fashioned hurricanes out of wind and sea, who invented leukemia, leprosy, Lou Gehrig's disease—why shouldn't this God suffer? He deserves far worse than three hours on a cross, and if He were to come back this very day, I swear to you, we'd kill Him all over again and be justified in doing so."

The archbishop tossed aside the *Review* and glared at me over his desk. I said that in my defense, he'd taken that quote out of context, to which he very nearly threw a punch, I believe, restraining himself at the last moment and taking a slow deep breath to regain his composure.

"Remind me," he said. "How long have you been a priest?"

I told him I didn't see how that was relevant.

"Twenty? Twenty-five years? You're old school, aren't you, Murphy? I bet you entered the seminary straight out of high school. Well, these days we encourage young men to wait a few years before joining. Go to college. Backpack through Europe. Experience the world. We consider it an important element of the discernment process, like dating other people before marrying the Church."

I didn't know where the archbishop was going with this. His anger I could understand, but he didn't seem angry anymore, or at least not as angry as he was a moment ago. He leaned back in his grand wooden chair and let his hands rest upon his belly like a man satisfied after a large meal. A ray of sunlight flashed over his episcopal ring. Gradually, a smile emerged on his face, and he even began to laugh softly, which was strangely terrifying.

"Murphy," he said, "it's good you're such an asshole. Otherwise it would be hard for me to tell you what it is I'm about to tell you."

I leaned forward, suddenly uncomfortable. Now that Marzano was out of the room, I'd expected screaming and crosier-shaking, something fire-and-brimstone-related, but none of these dramatics were forthcoming. The archbishop reached into his desk and produced a second document for my inspection. This was a thick, cream-colored sheet, the official stationary of the Archdiocese of Chicago. The top portion of the page was typed-out in a large gothic font. The bottom half displayed a series of signatures which belonged to the auxiliary bishops.

"Is this what I think it is?"

"An emergency tribunal was called earlier this morning."

"But I was under the impression—" The words caught in my throat. "I was under the impression that in such cases, the accused is given the opportunity to defend himself."

"Murphy, don't be an idiot. I've just given you that opportunity. But not only did you refuse to deny any part of Marzano's account, you showed absolutely no remorse in regards to your essay. If you ask me, I think you expected this to happen. I think deep down, you even wanted it. Well, if that's the case, then good riddance. I've never liked you, to be honest. You've always been an agitator, and this time you've gone too far. Now, since you clearly don't want any part of the Church, the Church has been forced to make it official. We don't want any part of you either."

I had no answer for this. My hands had begun to tremble around the sheet of Archdiocesan stationary, making it nearly impossible to read every line of the document. One word was painfully clear, though: *defrocked*.

"You should consider yourself lucky," said the archbishop. "In the old days, we'd burn heretics at the stake."

2

Thirty minutes later, I was in the car driving back to St. Peter's Catholic Church when my phone rang. It was my choir director, Charley Campbell.

"You disappeared on me," she said. "I get out of bed to fetch another bottle of wine, and when I come back, you're gone."

Reception isn't great on I-88 once you get outside the city, but it was good to hear her voice just then no matter how distant and broken it sounded. I imagined Charley as I had left her, de-robed and post-coital, buried under pages of script.

"Did you not like the first act?" she said. "Is that why you ran off?"

"Of course not. The first act is wonderful. You know that. Something just came up all of a sudden."

"Oh?"

"A theological emergency."

"What does that mean?"

The air thickened with the odor of manure as a big red truck pulling a cattle trailer passed me on the left.

"It means that the archbishop called and wanted to talk. But now that we're on the subject, I do think it could use some revision."

"I knew it. I knew you hated it."

Charley never took criticism well. We were halfway through a table reading of her latest play when I received the summons to his Grace's chamber. Honestly, I was grateful for the excuse to duck out.

"I assume you have a problem with the whole premise."

"Let's not put words in my mouth, okay?"

"But it's true. You aren't taking it seriously."

"Am I supposed to? I thought it was a comedy."

The sound of a disgruntled female artist crackled through the little earpiece on my phone. Charley's "magnum opus" (as she had referred to it, uncomfortably, at least three times while we were reading) was a screwball musical in which the US and Soviet Union coordinate a fake moon landing in order to divert all-out nuclear war. The play was called *One Small Step, One Giant Heap*, and sixty pages in, it was more than living up to its title.

"Sometimes I just want to strangle you, Leo."

"I never said I hated it."

"You didn't have to. The words are written all over your face."

I was just going to point out how ridiculous this statement was when Charley's antique typewriter began chopping out stage directions over the phone.

"Enter Fr. Leopold Murphy, 47, a once-handsome and vigorous man who over the last ten years has witnessed with heavy heart the steady decline of youth. His brow is wrinkled. His cheeks hang limp. His hair is thinning. There is winter in his beard."

It was like listening to a mechanical ice storm, all those strokes. I told Charley she'd made her point as I tried desperately to get around the cattle trailer.

"But it isn't the trappings of age that weigh most heavily on poor Murphy's heart. It's the impotence they signify."

"I don't remember you complaining earlier this afternoon."

"Suddenly, he spots Charley Campbell, 39, standing center stage, elegant, masterful, robed in a dark, flowing gown befitting Thalia, the ancient muse of comedy, her beauty rivaled only by her intense artistic genius. Murphy cowers before her like Actaeon before Artemis. Murphy (in moronic caveman voice): Me no get your play. Me think it stupid. Need more boom boom bang bang."

"Are you done? Do you have that out of your system?" I shut off the AC, hoping to stifle the smell of cow shit. The trailer had been in such a hurry to get around me, but now that it had me boxed in, it was going at least ten under. "Look, Charley, let me reserve judgment until we've read the thing all the way through. Then we can argue about it for as long as you want and have passionate make-up sex afterwards."

I accelerated like a teenager, whipping around the cattle and the big red truck, and shooting a nasty look at the driver as I sped by. He was an enormous, barrel-chested man with flabby c-cups and hair tufting out of all three holes of his wife-beater. He flipped me the bird and shouted what I lip-read to be, "Get off you're fucking phone, asshole," which is a pretty bold thing to shout at a man in clerics, defrocked or not.

"Charley? You still there?"

"Yeah."

"You still sore at me?"

"Yeah."

"You ever going to forgive me?"

"No."

I listened to the highway passing under my tires and thought of her, lying in my bed beside her typewriter. It was her most prized possession, a gift from her late grandmother who bought it at some big-shot publisher's estate sale when she visited London a few years before she died. The machine was rumored to once belong to Virginia Woolf (though, who are we kidding?) and thus held all sorts of mysterious, borderline voodoo, feminist/artistic sway over Charley, who's all-time favorite novel was, let's face it, *Mrs. Dalloway.*

"Can we read the rest of it tonight?" she said. "I'll order take-out. We won't have to leave the bedroom."

It physically hurt me to turn her down.

"Why not?"

"Because I'm having dinner with your husband this evening."

"Jesus."

"He asked me to be there with him for moral support. I didn't have the heart to tell him no."

"You're one great friend, you know that?"

"Let's not get catty."

"It's disgusting what he's doing," said Charley. "I don't care if it is for charity. There are other ways to raise money."

The road noise quieted to a gentle hum as I decelerated down the off ramp and then turned into the Alamo Steakhouse parking lot. I told Charley I'd arrived and would have to hang up now. I promised we'd read through the rest of her script just as soon as I was free.

"Leo, you never said what the archbishop wanted."

"Oh."

"The theological emergency?"

I didn't answer. The car was idling in the parking lot. The big neon sign for Alamo Steakhouse was blinking an electric-cow-blood's shade of red. A cartoon version of Davy Crockett was throwing a lasso over the horns of a huge Texas Steer.

"It wasn't anything serious, was it?"

I told her it was nothing, just some bureaucratic matter.

"You know I can always tell when you're lying."

"I know," I said, "but dammit I've really got to go. Seriously, I can hear the cows getting butchered from here. We'll talk later, okay?" I waited. "Okay?"

"Okay, Leo."

"Oh, and Charley?"

"Yes?"

"Don't read this morning's *St. John's Review*."

3

It always struck me as vaguely offensive that the kitchen and wait staff at Alamo Steakhouse was exclusively Mexican. Jerry Campbell was there at his regular table when I walked in, all three hundred and fifty pounds of him squeezed into the booth. He wore spurred leather boots, a black cowboy hat, and a massive white bib with the words "Beef Sherpa" emblazoned cattle-brand style over a pyramid built of hamburgers.

"So glad you could make it out, Murphy. José, get the father a menu, *por favor*."

"Right away, *Señor*."

"*Gracias*, José."

"Evening, Jerry," I said, squeezing into the booth opposite him. "What's with the getup?"

"Oh, these?" He tipped his hat and rattled his spurs as if he were the proudest cowhand in the West. "Just a little something they made me put on for the challenge."

He was referring to Ground Beef Mountain, the Alamo's famous trial of brass and gluttony in which a contestant (or, "Beef Sherpa") had one hour to consume twenty-five quarter-pounders or die trying. The prize for this Herculean feat included a burger-shaped trophy, a framed picture on the Alamo wall of fame, and ten thousand dollars cold hard cash, which might seem like an outrageous sum until you consider that of the sixty-four brave alpinist to have ever attempted Ground Beef Mountain, not one of them had reached the summit.

"You know, it isn't too late to back out of this. I think the kids would understand."

Jerry just grinned. I couldn't tell if that was a ketchup stain on his bib or dried blood. When José returned with the menu, I told him not to bother. I'd have a Caesar salad. He looked at me as if my ancestors had stolen his land and raped his women.

"You know there's no sharing, *Padre*. Señor Campbell must eat all those hamburgers himself or he doesn't get the *dinero*."

"I understand, José. I'll just have the Caesar salad."

"Bacon bits?"

"No thank you."

"Pulled pork?"

I shook my head.

"Some brisket shavings sprinkled over the top?"

"Just lettuce, dressing, and some croutons if it's not too much trouble."

José skulked back to the kitchen, muttering.

"So what's the plan here, Jerry? Ten thousand dollars, minus twenty-five hundred for bowel-reconstructive surgery, leaves an honest seventy-five for the children's hospital."

"That wouldn't be the worst case scenario."

"I see I'm not the only one who came to cheer you on."

A class of St. Peter's fourth graders had just entered the Alamo, ushered forward via three haggard-looking moms. The moment the kids spotted Jerry, they screamed with excitement and piled into the empty tables around us.

"You're an absolute saint," said one of the moms. The other two each gave Jerry a kiss on the cheek. José returned with my salad.

"Just a few more minutes, *Señor*."

14

Jerry tipped his cowboy hat and said, "Thank you, pilgrim," in what I guess was supposed to be a John Wayne impression. Now that it was here, I did wish there were bacon bits.

"Something the matter?"

"Hm?"

"You seem distant."

"Oh," I said.

Jerry was looking at me with genuine concern, but it was hard to take him seriously in his cowboy getup. Actually, it would've been hard to take him seriously even without the costume, because I'd been sleeping with his wife almost three years now, and he didn't have the slightest clue. It was like we were acting out one of those Chaucerian fabliaux where the clergy are always running around, seducing the town idiot's bombshell girlfriend. Charley and I had become so brazen with our "table readings," I sometimes daydreamed about just what stunts of sexual mischief we could get away with. There was one fantasy in particular which involved me sneaking into her bedroom late one night and riding her like a bucking steer while Jerry sawed logs right next to us. It was the trail of cartoon z's and the image of cuckold's horns curling up from his sleeping cap that really brought the whole scene to life.

"Maybe you could use a vacation."

"What are you talking about?"

"I don't know. You just seem down these days. Not as happy as you used to be."

Jerry's moments of perception, though rare, never failed to unnerve me. I crunched some lettuce and thought of Jesus up there on the cross, you know, getting what he deserved.

"Which reminds me," he said. "I just discovered something interesting." He reached into his pocket and produced a folded-up travel brochure. The company was Paradise Cruise Lines, the destination San Juandigo.

"Hold on. This isn't…."

"No, it's legit," he insisted. "I've done a ton of research, and the resort's still standing, still operational. They're even offering a discount because of, well…"

"The earthquake?"

Jerry nodded.

I shook my head, wondering why the hell anyone would want to spend their vacation kicking around the rubble of some tropical slum. San Juandigo was a tiny island in the south Caribbean that had recently suffered a major earthquake, crippling its infrastructure and leaving nearly half its population without running water or electricity. I'd heard through the grapevine that my brother, Stephen, a man with more money than sense, had already traveled there to do humanitarian work along with his special brand of evangelization. Meanwhile, one of the St. Peter's fourth graders had seen a segment about the disaster on BBC's *World News*, and within days, the crazy idea had spread through the school to send a class down to rebuild a children's hospital which had toppled over in the earthquake. For almost a month now, the kids had been hawking coupon books and chalky candy bars trying to raise money for airfare. It was Jerry (already a folk hero thanks to his famous good spirits and Paul Bunyan-esque girth) who had the idea to tackle Ground Beef Mountain.

"You remember how Charley and I missed out on a proper honeymoon. She's always wanted to travel, but we've never had the money. This would still take a couple of years to save up for, but at least it's something."

I leaned over the table and whispered so that none of the fourth graders would hear.

"You know, Jerry, you could always just screw the children's hospital and pocket that ten grand for yourself."

He laughed a big, wobbling, fat-man's laugh. I guess he thought I was kidding.

16

"Unfortunately, that would only get us one ticket, and I'm pretty sure my wife would be upset if I didn't tag along."

Our friendship was so rife with dramatic irony, a sentence like that didn't even faze me.

"*Señors y Señoras*, may I have your attention, *por favor*."

José emerged from the kitchen, ringing one of those big brass bells they use for boxing matches. The room fell silent. Everyone in Alamo Steakhouse, and I mean everyone, not just the fourth graders and the three moms, looked over to see what was up.

"It is my honor to present Señor Campbell, bravest of all *hombres*."

The kids from Saint Peter's started cheering, their excitement spreading like wildfire through the restaurant until everyone at the Alamo was clapping and whooping and yelling out encouragement. Jerry tipped his hat to all those assembled. José set aside the boxing bell and pulled out an electric stop watch to count down the allotted sixty minutes. When the doors to the kitchen swung open, a hush fell over the room.

"Sweet Jesus," said Jerry.

"Oh my goodness," said one of the moms.

"There must be twenty pounds of cow on that plate," said a man with Sweet n' Smoky BBQ sauce smeared across his cheeks.

It was just like 1836 all over again: poor Davy Crockett and the boys staring down that huge Mexican army getting ready to slaughter them. Ground Beef Mountain was enormous, like *actual mountain* enormous. Twenty-five quarter pounders, hot off the grill and still dripping in their own fat, composed a pyramid of meat, bun, lettuce, tomato, caramelized onion, and Alamo Steakhouse BBQ Sauce that required two burly cooks (muscles straining) to heft out of the kitchen and carry up to our booth.

"That's some dinner," I said to Jerry. "You really think you can eat all that?"

"You can do it!" shouted one of the fourth graders. "Show those burgers who's boss!"

The sentiment was echoed many times over while José set the electric stopwatch down on the table and pulled out some sort of legal document for Jerry to sign.

"What's that?" I said. "Your last will and testament?"

He laughed again and handed the document back to José. "Just something to protect the restaurant. You know, so Charley can't sue if I die."

"Jesus Christ, are you for real?"

"Don't worry. José assured me that beef-related fatalities are extremely rare."

"But people *have* actually expired trying to do this?"

"Okay, so it's medium rare."

I told Jerry it wasn't funny. What the hell was I supposed to tell Charley if something happened to him?

He just grinned at me through a hole in the pyramid and tipped his hat one last time. "Tell her that I went out doing what I love. She'll understand."

This is exactly what I hated about Jerry. He was always so goddamn happy and optimistic about things and for no good reason at all. I mean, just look at the man. He was fat, ugly, poor, he worked a shitty job, the woman he loved more than anything in the world was cheating on him with his best friend. If I were in his place, I'd march right over to the gun store and put a bullet through my head. But Jerry wasn't despondent at all. In fact he was downright joyful. It was disgusting.

"Señor Campbell, are you ready?"

"Let's do this thing, José."

"Then begin!"

Everyone started cheering as Jerry tore into his first burger. I'll spare you the gorier details, but let's just say not everything made it cleanly down the gullet. A line of grease thickened with Sweet n' Smokey arced over the pyramid and into my Caesar salad, which I promptly pushed aside. It was thrashing

18

teeth and beef chunks everywhere. I felt like I was back in ancient Rome watching Christians getting torn apart by lions. He polished off four burgers in two minutes flat. Prefontaine would call that a suicide pace, but Jerry just kept swallowing. He ate with an animal's pleasure, like a pig smiling into his bucket of slops.

"Excuse me," I said, sliding out of the booth. "I need to visit the restroom."

Jerry didn't look up. I'm not sure he even heard me over the crowd noise. I squeezed past the tables of fourth graders and headed to the other side of the Alamo where big, hand-painted signs designated the facilities for "Cowboys" and "Cowgirls," respectively. You had to push through a pair of saloon doors to get inside, and there was sawdust on the ground instead of tile, and a long, piss-stained trough where the urinals were traditionally located. Still, it was nice to get away from all the chaos for a moment. I splashed some water on my face and then checked to make sure no one was in the stalls. Then I took my phone out and called Charley.

"That was quick. Did he finish already, or is he passed out in some hospital room with a BBQ sauce I.V.?"

"Neither," I told her. "Not yet, at least."

"What? You aren't there for moral support?"

"I just needed to step out a moment. The whole situation was making me nauseous."

"Ah."

"Teeth and burgers and grease-soaked buns."

"Okay, no need to get graphic."

"I'm talking serious carnage."

"I can imagine."

"Listen, Charley, the reason I'm calling…" I looked at my reflection in the mirror and tried to picture it without the collar. "Well, it's about my meeting today with the archbishop. Something big happened. Something I need to talk to you about."

19

The saloon doors swung open, and in stepped the man with Sweet n' Smokey on his cheeks, his gut extending a good fourteen inches past his belt. While he unzipped over the trough, I pretended to order a pizza, which in retrospect didn't make much sense. Luckily Mr. Sweet n' Smokey—drifting in and out of what I could only assume to be a stage-1 beef coma—was in no state to be suspicious.

"Lord, that man can put 'em away," he said, fumbling blindly for his cock. I didn't know if he was talking to me specifically or to the universe in general. Once he got a hold of the thing, he peed like a race horse. "I thought *I* could eat, but that guy, that guy's got an appetite. I bet he'd scarf down God's green earth if you put it on a plate for him."

The man zipped up and washed himself at the sink. The moment he was gone, I told Charley to hold on a second while I checked on her husband. Jerry was fifteen minutes in and still going strong. Ground Beef Mountain, now peak-less and with a serious dent in its north face, was a mere shadow of its former self, though one couldn't help but think all those quarter-pounders still had some fight left in them.

"He's got a ways to go," I told her. I went back through the saloon doors into a space of relative peace and quiet. The sawdust did a good job dampening whatever crowd noise got through the walls. I took a breath before asking what it was I wanted to ask. "Say, Charley, what would you think about moving to New York and giving your playwriting career a real shot?"

She laughed at me through the phone.

"I'm serious."

"Don't be cruel. You know that ship has sailed. Besides, you don't even like my magnum opus."

"Yeah, but what do I know? I'm not a playwright or an agent. I don't own a Broadway theater."

"You were going to tell me what happened this afternoon with the archbishop."

20

I made a little hole in the sawdust with my foot. I thought about how beautiful Charley was and how much I cared for her. I know I joke about cuckold's horns and Chaucerian fabliaux and all that, but honestly our relationship was more than just lechery. Charley was one of the few good things left in my life. I loved her, I think, and I think she loved me, too. Or at least I hoped she did.

"Run away with me," I said.

"What?"

"I want you to leave Jerry and come with me to New York. I'll get a job teaching theology. You can write your plays. We'll live the life you've always dreamed of living."

"What are you talking about, Leo? Where's all this coming from?"

I took another breath to compose myself. Then I told her everything that had happened that afternoon. It felt good to get it out of my system. It was like a purge. I instantly felt ten pounds lighter.

"But what does that mean, 'defrocked'? You won't be the pastor at St. Peter's anymore?"

"I won't be the pastor anywhere. I won't be a priest at all."

"All because of an essay?"

"That's right."

"Seems a little extreme, doesn't it?"

"Well…"

"I mean, what exactly did you write that they'd kick you out of the Church?"

"First of all, they didn't kick me out of the Church. I'm defrocked, not excommunicated. And second, what I said in the essay isn't important right now. Charley, I need to know if you'll come with me. I understand this is all very sudden and a lot to think about, but I'm actually starting to believe this whole thing was ultimately for the best."

Silence on the other end of the line. Through the restroom walls, I heard a big cheer from the Saint Peter's fourth graders.

21

I poked my head out and saw that Jerry was about twelve burgers in with thirty-five minutes to go. He was still keeping a good pace, but you could tell the meat was starting to get to him. He was sweating like a pig under that cowboy hat. José stood nearby, refilling his water and occasionally dabbing his brow with a napkin. Everyone else in the restaurant had stopped eating. Half-devoured rib racks and loaded baked potatoes sat unattended on Alamo Steakhouse platters. A ring of spectators had formed around Jerry's booth, causing the fourth graders (who, being fourth graders, were all pretty short) to abandon their chairs and stand atop the tables to watch the action. The three moms looked on (concerned) but ultimately said nothing. One of them was standing on a table herself.

"You can do it, *Señor*," said José.

"You can do it, Jerry," said the table-perched mom.

I imagined all those children kicking around in the rubble of San Juandigo and wondered what they would think of this man eating his heart out for their sake. Did they even care about the hospital? Maybe they'd rather have all those quarter-pounders.

"Are you still there?"

"I'm still here, Charley. I was just checking on the progress."

"How's he doing?"

"It's going to be a nail-biter."

"Listen, Leo, about New York, I just don't know. Jerry and I have been together for a long time, and now, completely out of the blue, you ask me to quit my job, leave my husband, say goodbye to all my friends, and move halfway across the country? You know I have feelings for you, but you're expecting kind of a lot here. When I saw your name pop up on my phone, I thought you were calling to apologize for being so critical of my play."

I closed my eyes and tried to picture Charley sitting at a desk in our new Manhattan apartment. She wore dark, sexy

22

glasses and had her hair pulled up into a loose bun just how I liked it. She was pounding away at Virginia Woolf's old typewriter while a Bob Dylan record accompanied the clatter of keys. Whenever she finished a page, she would tear it from the machine and pass it over to the bed where I was lying, bare-chested, a glass of red wine in one hand and the folded-up Arts section of the *New York Times* in the other. "What's the word?" she would ask me, and I would laugh and kiss her and tell her how everyone was raving over her latest play.

"Leo? Hello? Leo?"

"Charley, listen to me. When I met with the archbishop this afternoon, it occurred to me that I need to experience things in a new light. In fact, I think we *both* could use some new light."

"I still don't know."

"Why?"

"I just don't."

"But why?"

"Because you're the one who got defrocked, not me."

The room suddenly fell silent, accentuating her words in a heavy-handed directorial kind of way. I poked my head out through the saloon doors to find out what was up, but the crowd around Jerry was so thick, I couldn't see him.

"Leo?"

"Got to go, Charley. Something's happened."

I hung up on her and then pushed my way through the spectators back to our booth, not an easy task considering the girth of your average Alamo Steakhouse patron. Jerry was right there where I had left him, his black cowboy hat hanging so low I couldn't see anything above his mouth. That mouth, by the way, was still chewing, albeit much more slowly now and with a forced, almost grinding weariness, like an old motor sans oil.

"What's going on here? Status report, José."

"Not good, *Padre*. The mountain, it is unconquerable."

23

Jerry had done some real topographic damage. Of the original twenty-five burgers, only about ten remained. They composed a single layer of foundation nowhere near as daunting as the complete structure but still more than any reasonable human being would consume. The surviving burgers were far from appetizing. Having borne the weight of Ground Beef Mountain for almost three quarters of an hour, they were flattened and completely grease-soaked. Even the top buns were soggy, like patties of oatmeal cooked in lard.

"How's it going, Jerry? You feeling alright?"

He didn't answer, just kept chewing in that slow, defeated way of his. Lines of BBQ sauce ran from the edges of his lips, down his jaw, and over his many chins.

"Maybe you should throw in the towel, big guy. Everyone's looking pretty worried here. No shame in giving up."

He was perspiring freely. His bib was a Jackson Pollack of sauce and grease and sweat.

"Seriously, Jerry, you're starting to scare the kids."

I felt a hand on my shoulder.

"It's no use, *Padre*. He's made his decision."

"What the hell are you talking about, José?"

The Mexican shook his head. "It's him or the mountain now. There can only be *uno*."

The stopwatch sitting on the table showed that Jerry had fifteen minutes remaining, which meant that if those poor kids down in San Juandigo were going to get their hospital rebuilt, he would need to average just under a burger a minute. He finished the one in his mouth and picked up another, grease dripping like rainwater off the bottom bun. It was obvious to everyone that he was in real pain now, but what was there to do? Like José said, he had made his decision. He was going to see this through to the end, one way or the other.

4

The day I met Jerry Campbell was a Friday during Lent about fifteen years ago. I remember because he was eating a McDonald's fish fillet sandwich, which he never did (on account of the indigestion) except when the Church asked him to. It was a cold Friday, as I recall. A mid-February chilliness hung in the air. The sky was no longer the depressing shade of grey it had been for so many weeks, but you still couldn't venture outside without a jacket, unless you were Jerry, in which case you had your own personal layer of blubber with you at all times.

"You must be the new pastor," he said, offering a hand sticky with tartar sauce. "I'm Jerry Campbell, the groundskeeper here."

"Leopold Murphy."

He looked at me queerly over his parabolic chins. Late morning sunlight, not exactly warm, but at least bright, shone across half his face, revealing crumbs of fried breading at the corners of his lips. We were standing in the parking lot directly between St. Peter's church and St. Peter's grade school. All the spaces reserved for faculty cars were full. It was recess time, so a group of students was playing kickball about a hundred yards away on a baseball diamond without bases or pitching mound.

"Leopold," said Jerry. "Now that's an unusual name."

"My father's doing. He was kind of obsessed with James Joyce's *Ulysses*."

"Ah, *Ulysses*. I haven't gotten around to that one yet. My wife, Charley, now she's more of the literary type."

"Is that so?"

"Oh, yeah, a regular bookworm." He balled up the wrapper from his fish fillet and slipped it into his pocket. "Well, shall we?"

Jerry had volunteered to show me around St. Peter's and introduce me to everyone I should know. This was just my second church since receiving orders. I'd spent the previous ten years at St. Raphael's on the south side of Chicago, serving the poor Hispanics and blacks of the area with the bulletproof idealism found only in the newly ordained. Now I'd been given a new challenge. Starting today, I was to take over as pastor of this relatively young church about an hour outside the city in a place called Chippewa County, which had, I swear, more strip malls than persons of color. Just fifteen minutes into the tour, and I could already tell things were going to be different. Jerry showed me the school first. He introduced me to the principal (a warm, chipper forty-something white woman) and a few of the teachers (warm, chipper, twenty-something white women). Next we saw the cafeteria, the gymnasium, and the newly-constructed theater, then the classrooms that instead of chalkboards had these big, interactive computer screens that you could write on with special computer markers.

"Pretty cool, huh?"

"Looks expensive," I said.

The church was architecturally very impressive. Neo-gothic, I believe you would call it. The word "church" doesn't actually do the thing justice. "Cathedral" or "basilica" seems more appropriate. Huge stone columns and vaulted ceilings, rows upon rows of wooden pews, a bloody crucifix hanging over the altar, oil paintings for all fourteen Stations of the Cross. The setting took me back to my younger days at St.

26

Ignatius High School where the old Jesuits made us suffer through the Sacrament of Reconciliation at least once a quarter. Just walking through the place made me feel guilty for masturbating.

"Do you want to see the bell tower?" said Jerry. "It's my job to ring the bell."

We climbed the steep, dark, twisting steps. When we reached the top, it was actually quite pleasant. Sunlight poured through the open windows and over the big, brass church bell hanging in the center of the room. It was cold up here, but not uncomfortably so. The tower overlooked a rich suburbscape of manicured lawns and newly-planted oak trees. There was an eighteen-hole golf course and a park with racquetball and tennis courts. Chippewa County was beautiful from this distance.

"Can you see Charley down there?"

"Hm?"

"Look," said Jerry. He leaned over the window and pointed out a young woman kneeling in the garden just below us. "She's getting ready to plant the spring flowers."

"That's your wife?"

"Yes, sir. Married four and a half years to the day."

I watched Charley push a hand spade into the earth and turn the cold soil. She was kneeling on one of those foam gardener's pads and had her hair tied back in a pony-tail over her shoulder. She wore loose and comfortable clothing: a white button down, a jacket pulled over which she didn't mind getting dirty. The way she held her tools and worked the ground, you could tell there was no place in the world she'd rather be.

"She's beautiful," I said to Jerry. "Does she work here?"

"Choir director, though her real passion's the theater."

"You don't say?"

"She's a playwright. You should read some of her stuff. It's good, you know. A bit over my head." He gave me a sly grin

27

from the window. "I know what you're thinking, Fr. Murphy. You're wondering how a girl like that ever wound up with a guy like me."

"Honestly, the thought did cross my mind."

He laughed boisterously and slapped my shoulder. His hands were warm and meaty, like steaks. "I know I'm no movie star or NFL quarterback or brilliant nuclear physicist."

I waited for the second half of that sentence while he called down to his wife. Charley looked up from the garden and waved.

"I hope she plants zucchini again this year. Usually she just plants flowers, but sometimes she sneaks in a vegetable or two. They're always delicious."

"I'm sorry, was that it?"

"Hm?"

"Your explanation."

Jerry looked at me. He still had that big dumb grin on his face. "What were we talking about again?"

5

We were talking about pain: serious, gut-wrenching pain. Everyone could feel it. The whole Alamo Steakhouse was one burger-stuffed node of empathy. The stopwatch on the table read eight minutes remaining, and there were only four quarter-pounders left on the plate. No one had said a word in at least five minutes. The entire staff (this includes the hostess, the grill masters, even Earl, the restaurant manager with his khaki slacks and red polo shirt and gold-plated nametag) was gathered around the booth to watch Jerry suffer. He picked up burger *numero* four and bit into it. One good thing about the grease puddle was that it had substantially broken down all that organic tissue. Jerry, I'm sure, was battling through some serious tendonitis of the jaw, but his teeth passed right through those burgers no problem. It was hard to even differentiate the ingredients at this point. Meat, bun, lettuce, tomato, onion—all had melded together, resulting in a brown, gelatinous mass of protein. I feared what horrors were transpiring inside his stomach, and it occurred to me that I no longer had the authority to administer extreme unction.

"That's it, *Señor*," said José, who'd been whispering the Rosary in Spanish. "You must believe. You must have faith. Only with God's help can you ever hope to defeat the mountain."

But even God couldn't help Jerry now. He swallowed in agony. The quarter-pounder didn't make it to his stomach. It stopped at the base of his throat, no place left for it to go. Even if I'd wanted to step away, I couldn't now. The booth was surrounded. The St. Peter's fourth graders had climbed down from the tables and were kneeling before Jerry like supplicants at the altar. The desire in their eyes was an absurd desire, but it was pure and selfless nonetheless. This was too much to ask of a man, I wanted to say. And this was no place for children. But the moment was beyond my power. Jerry pushed the third burger into his mouth. He bit and chewed and swallowed. He bit and chewed and swallowed.

"Five minutes," cried José.

"This is going to kill him."

"You can do it, Señor Campbell."

"Doesn't anyone see this is going to kill him?"

"*Padre?*"

"I said this is going to kill him. You hear that, Jerry? This is going to kill you."

A gasp rippled through the Alamo. José crossed himself. The fourth-graders all looked up at me, frightened.

"This whole thing is insane," I said. "Someone should stop this. It isn't safe."

Jerry finished the third quarter-pounder and without pausing, without even acknowledging my outburst, started work on the penultimate burger. You still couldn't see his eyes because of that fucking ridiculous cowboy hat.

"I can't in good conscience sit here and let you do this. You're an idiot, Jerry. You go through life like a big dumb fool, which would be fine if there weren't people in this world who cared about you."

He didn't stop. He just kept eating.

"When are you going to realize it isn't worth it, huh? Ten thousand dollars for a new hospital? Shit, there's just going to be another earthquake in like a week."

30

"*Padre*, the children."

"And if there isn't, then what? All those kids with their horrible diseases, I'll let you in on a little secret, they're going to die anyway. So why bother? Why put yourself through this?"

There was only one burger left, a single patty floating in a lake of grease. Jerry picked it up and brought it to his mouth.

"That's it, Señor Campbell. Chew. Chew."

"Chew! Chew! Chew!" chanted the St. Peter's fourth graders.

"Chew! Chew! Chew!" chanted the Alamo Steakhouse employees.

"Chew! Chew! Chew!" chanted literally everyone in the restaurant sans me and Jerry.

The final quarter-pounder, *numero* twenty-five of twenty-five, passed through his mouth and settled halfway down his throat. A cheer swept over the Alamo. Jerry fell face first into his plate. A big meaty splash. The rim of his cowboy hat darkened with grease.

"*Dios mío*," said José.

Jerry Campbell was dead.

6

Whenever someone died in Chippewa County, the bereaved had two options in regards to mortuary services. There was O'Brian's Funeral Home located on the west side of town at Cherry and Pine, and there was O'Brian's Funeral Parlor located on the east side of town at Redwood and Maple. The houses were owned and operated by Roger and Damian O'Brian, rival homosexual morticians whom everyone in Chippewa County affectionately referred to as the Brothers Grimm. Since St. Peter's was closer to the east side, Charley employed Damian to handle the wake, and so it was on a Tuesday night, just days after the incident at Alamo Steakhouse, that I pulled into the parking lot of O'Brian's Funeral Parlor and discovered a line of mourners stretching clear past the doors.

"Sure are a lot of cold people out here," said Roger O'Brian, tapping his alligator-skin dress shoes impatiently on the sidewalk. "I suppose Mrs. Campbell should've picked an establishment with more capacity. Hope there's coffee inside, or would that be too much to expect?"

I told him Charley went with his brother because he was closer, it wasn't anything personal, to which Roger examined his cufflinks and said (with sass befitting his sexual orientation) that a ditch on the side of the road might be *closer*, but that didn't necessarily make it an acceptable alternative. "Mrs. Campbell's lucky I owe her husband my life. Otherwise, I might not have shown up this evening."

This was a pretty heartbreaking thing to hear if you knew the context like I did. For the past ten or eleven years, Roger and Jerry had been going to a therapy group for men struggling to conceive (as in, sexually). The group met on Monday nights at eight o'clock in the basement of St. Peter's and included anywhere between five and twenty guys, depending on whether or not the Bears were playing on Monday Night Football. I'd never actually attended one of these things myself, but from what Jerry told me, they consisted of a group of men with bum sperm or else married to wives with bum tubes sitting around in a circle, drinking coffee, and talking about how empty their lives were without children. Jerry, I should note, never indulged his disappointment quite like the others. Sure, he would've welcomed a couple rug rats scampering around the house, and yes, maybe he didn't quite understand why that wasn't part of "God's plan" for him, but like he told me once, life with Charley was a blessing, procreation or not.

For Roger O'Brian, by contrast, one couldn't help but believe these weekly meetings were the only thing standing between him and a garageful of carbon monoxide. He and his brother, Damian, had apprenticed together at their dad's funeral parlor ever since they were little boys. The old man wanted only two things in life: for his children to grow up to be the best morticians in Chippewa County and for a grandson to pass on the family name. Unfortunately, that second wish was complicated by that fact that both Damian and Roger were gay, which didn't stop either of them from marrying and then eventually divorcing a series of desperate women. In the last throes of his final marriage, Roger befriended Jerry through conception therapy, and one night, when it was their turn to

33

stay late and put away the chairs, he confessed that he and his wife were no longer intimate.

"I'm sorry to hear that," said Jerry. "I really am. I know everybody's got these jokes about sex being worth it, kids or not, but sometimes it just seems pointless. It's like with me and Charley. Okay, so we love each other, and this is how people in love express that, but sometimes it feels like there's something more we're missing out on, like we're broken somehow, and if we could just get fixed then everything would be one hundred percent better."

"That's really brave and honest of you to say that, Jerry, and I want you to know I appreciate your openness, or whatever we're supposed to say in group, but to tell you the truth, I'm talking about something completely different."

"Oh?" Jerry looked up from the trashcan where he'd just dumped the coffee grounds and a stack of Styrofoam cups. "What do you mean?"

So Roger O'Brian explained to Jerry how he and his brother were homosexuals and how they'd been living these false parallel lives in hopes of pleasing their father and how the only reason they were such bitter rivals via the funeral business was because that was the only venue in which either of them could ever hope to succeed.

"Wow," said Jerry. "That's a lot to keep bottled up." He was thinking about Roger's original phrase, "no longer intimate," and was wondering if that meant he and his soon-to-be-ex-wife actually *had been* intimate at some point, in which case, what exactly were the mechanics of a situation like that?

"Anyway," said Roger, "I just wanted you to know the truth. On the one hand, I think you deserve to know, since you're a stand-up guy, Jerry, not to mention the only real friend I've made here. On the other hand, I wanted to tell you because if I have to carry this around with me any longer, pretending everything's fine and dandy except for my 'bum sperm situation,' then I'm afraid I might just do something really desperate. You know, as in *fatally* desperate."

"Oh," said Jerry. "Well in that case, I'm glad you told me."

"I'm glad I told you, too," said Roger.

Police officers and Catholic priests have no problem jumping line when there's a body involved, so I told Roger I had to go find someone inside and then made my way through the main hall and into the room where Jerry was being displayed. There I spotted Charley, black-dressed and puffy-eyed, receiving condolences next to a big poster with pictures of her and her late husband. I waited until she was alone before approaching.

"Good evening, Fr. Murphy, thank you for coming."

"May I speak to you in private, Charley? I feel like there's a lot we need to discuss."

She looked away, fighting back tears, or I don't know, maybe the urge to slap me. We hadn't talked since Jerry's death, though I'd left her countless messages.

"At least let me give you this. It's the ten thousand dollars from the restaurant. They pass along their deepest sympathies, by the way."

She wouldn't take the money.

"Come on."

"I don't want it. Keep it away from me. Besides, that's for the children's hospital."

I looked around to make sure no one was listening. Then I spoke in a whisper only the widow could hear. "Look, everyone knows Jerry didn't have much in terms of savings or insurance. The kids will understand if you hold onto this."

She didn't respond.

"I know it's an incredibly stressful time right now, but you have to be reasonable."

"And what would you have me do? Take that ten grand and run off to New York with you? Rent some crappy apartment for three months so we can screw and read plays?"

"Charley, keep your voice down."

"Why? You're not a priest anymore. There are no appearances to keep up."

"People are staring."

"Good. Let them stare. I want them to stare. We could both use some public shaming for what we've done. You've been a horrible friend, and I've been a horrible wife, and together we killed a man who only ever wished good things for us."

Before the scene could escalate further, I took Charley by the hand and led her roughly out of the room.

"Let go of me," she snapped. "I swear I'll scream."

I told her she was being hysterical and that she should stop embarrassing herself.

"Where are you taking me? Back to your place? That's a right gentlemanly thing to do, sleeping with the widow on the night of her husband's wake."

"We're not going to have sex. We're just going to talk. Now will you please get a hold of yourself and step outside with me for a moment?"

We were standing in the parlor's main hall, an elegant, lushly-carpeted space with soft, yellow lamps and mahogany chairs. Everyone waiting to pay their last respects to Jerry was looking at us, expect for Roger O'Brian who was examining a sailboat painting on the wall and making critical clicking noises with his tongue.

"Charley, please." I held open the back door. "I'm just asking for five minutes."

7

Three years earlier, we were out in a snowstorm on the St. Peter's parking lot, hunched over her car, trying to get the damn thing to start. It was late, maybe ten or eleven o'clock. I'd been stuck in a finance meeting all night, and Charley had just finished up choir practice. Everyone else was gone, which was a problem since neither of us knew anything about auto mechanics.

"Well, I have to think it's the battery," I said.

"The battery, huh?"

"Yeah, I'm pretty sure it's the battery."

We were doing that thing people do, standing over the car with the hood popped open, hoping the problem would just come out and announce itself. Snowflakes fell wet and heavy over the exposed engine. I touched one of the hoses to make sure it wasn't loose.

"Do you mind giving me a jump?" said Charley. "I think I've got the cables in the back."

While she dug out the equipment, I pulled my car around and popped open the hood. It was really coming down at this point. The snow had climbed four or five inches up Charley's tires. Our cars were starting to look like mobile igloos.

"Well, here they are."

"Yep, those are the cables, all right."

37

"So what's the next step?"

"You know, Mrs. Campbell, this is embarrassing, but I don't have the faintest idea."

"Really?"

"Sorry."

Cold and defeated, Charley and I sought shelter in the principal's office. While she called her husband, I took a seat at the table where earlier that evening, I and nine members of the board of trustees had argued for, I don't know, let's say thirteen hours, over plans for St. Peter's new state-of-the-art playground, which was either going to cost one hundred and twenty thousand dollars or one hundred and forty thousand dollars depending on whether we sprung for 100% recycled materials, which everyone agreed was a lot better for the environment and probably a good first step in reversing the catastrophic effects of climate change, but let's be real, an extra twenty large was an extra twenty large.

About midway through the debate (so this was like hour six, let's assume), I had the audacity to suggest that perhaps one hundred and twenty thousand dollars (the "cheap" option) was kind of a lot to spend on a see-saw and some swings. Maybe all that money would do more good if it were reallocated to the church's poor fund, seeing as Jesus had a lot to say regarding poverty while remaining essentially mute on the topic of jungle gyms. At which point one of the board members quoted Matthew 19:14, "Let the children come to me. [Jesus] Do not stop them, for the kingdom of Heaven belongs to them," and said that he would be damned if St. Peter's didn't take JC's message to heart and build the best, greenest, most children-welcoming playground in all of Chippewa County, to hell with the checkbook.

And then one of the other board members piped up, "Now hold on. What do you mean, 'to hell with the checkbook?' I'm all for the kingdom of Heaven, but how about some fiscal responsibility?"

38

And then somebody else countered with, "Give unto Caesar what is Caesar's," which didn't really make a whole lot of sense in context, but did prove effective in re-sparking a fresh and vigorous debate. By the end of hour thirteen, when exhaustion and phone calls from angry wives brought things to a close, we'd made essentially no progress vis-à-vis the playground. We had, however, passed a few common-sense measures limiting the quoting of Holy Scripture during financial debates, and so all things considered, it was one of our more productive meetings.

"Hey, Jerry, it's me. I guess you went to bed early, but I was just calling to let you know the car died, and that I'm still up at St. Peter's."

As Charley explained the situation to her husband's voicemail, I went to the window and slid open the blinds. It wasn't looking good out there. Six, maybe seven inches of powder. A layer of freezing rain under that. I had to imagine the roads were a mess.

"I'm just going to call a tow truck, if that's okay."

"Go ahead," I told her, "though I doubt they'll be able to make it out in this storm."

I was right. The old guy working the graveyard shift at Leroy's passed along his sincerest apologies but explained that given the present conditions, it was simply impossible to come get her.

"Well, shit," said Charley. "What do I do now?"

"Bunker down 'till spring?"

"No offense, Fr. Murphy, but you haven't been much help this evening."

"I already told you I was embarrassed about the jumper cables. No need to rub it in."

Charley joined me at the window, and we watched the snow come down in silence for some time. In a strange way, it was actually comforting once we gave up all hope of escape. I imagine the dead feel a similar relief.

"You know," said Charley, "I saw a story on the news once about this order of nuns. The pope was coming to visit their convent for some reason. I don't remember why. They lived in this really beautiful area, and they wanted the pope to say a mass outside, surrounded by nature. The only problem was he was visiting right in the middle of the rainy season, which was usually welcomed by the nuns—the rainy season—because they had a vineyard and winery where they made communion wine for a whole bunch of churches, but in this instance, the rain was more of an inconvenience than anything else."

"You saw this on the news, you said?"

"I don't know. Maybe it was a movie. I can't remember. The point is, these nuns decided the best thing to do was pray for good weather. And they really took it seriously, the praying, as in day and night, 24/7. Don't look at me like that. It's true. They prayed in shifts. They knelt before the altar. They thumbed their rosaries. All the while, they contemplated draughts and deserts and empty blue skies. I think they even tore the pages with the story of Noah's Ark out of all their Bibles, or maybe that's an apocryphal detail I just now invented." She paused a moment to mouth-breathe some fog on the cold window. With the tip of her index finger, she drew a little storm cloud with raindrops underneath. "And that's how the convent operated for let's say six or seven months, all the way up to the morning of the pope's visit."

"Did it work?"

"Well, funny thing," said Charley. "It did work, only too well. When the pope arrived, halleluiah, there wasn't a cloud to be seen. He visited the convent, took a grand tour of the vineyards, said a beautiful mass in the midst of God's glorious creation. And then he left, and then a week passed and it didn't rain, and then two weeks passed and it didn't rain, and then a month, and then three months, and then wouldn't you know it, the convent suffered through the worst draught on record. Most of the grapevines died. Those that didn't produced these shriveled bitter raisins that were not only a bitch to smash up, excuse the language, but also made just about the worst wine you ever tasted. Churches couldn't use the stuff. It was like actually drinking Jesus' blood. So without the money they always counted on from the winery, the nuns went bankrupt and had to sell their land, and pretty soon they were all living out on the street right next to the beggars they once served. You know what? I just remembered this wasn't a news story or a movie. It was a play I wrote in college when I was studying to be the next great American playwright. It was called *The Convent of St. Bernadette: A Tragic Case of Getting What You Wish For*, and if I recall correctly, it was ripped apart—I mean absolutely shredded—in workshop."

"Hm," I said, not looking directly at Charley, but at her reflection in the window through which I could still see the snow falling over the parking lot. "I think the point of that story, and by that I mean both the play and your retelling of it just now, has to do with the frustration one feels when attempting to impose order upon a seemingly disordered universe. The nuns are like us in that we all find ourselves essentially agentless in the face of great and unthinking power (ie. the weather), and any attempts to control this power, or even influence it, are in the long run completely ineffective."

"No," said Charley. "You've completely misunderstood. The reason I told you that story is because I want you to pray to God and ask Him to make it stop snowing so that I can go home and sleep in my own bed tonight."

"Oh, well, in that case, you shouldn't have been so passive-aggressive about it."

She clicked her nails slowly against the window. Then she looked at me. "You know what I could really use right now?"

"A shovel?"

"A drink."

And that's how around midnight we ended up in the faculty lounge sipping eggnog spiked with whiskey and watching the second half of *It's a Wonderful Life* on the TV they had in there so that the teachers could keep up on their soaps. I had my shoes off and my collar out, and Charley was curled up next to me on the couch, and both of us, I could tell, were feeling a whole lot more comfortable with each other now that we had a few cups of nog in us.

"May I ask you a personal question, Mrs. Campbell?"

"Certainly," she said, "but on one condition."

"What's that?"

"You have to call me Charley from now on."

"Okay."

"Because we've known each other for more than ten years, and whenever you say Mrs. Campbell, it makes me feel like an old woman with cats at home and plastic on the furniture and hard, unpleasant caramels in the candy dish which no one ever eats."

"Alright, Charley, but if that's the case, then you can't call me Fr. Murphy anymore either."

"Then what should I call you? *Leopold*?"

"What? You don't like that?"

"How about just Leo?"

"Perfect," I told her. "And now that we have that settled, what I wanted to ask is how the hell a woman like you ended up with a man like Jerry, no offense?"

"Oh," said Charley.

She took another drink from her eggnog. We were drinking out of Styrofoam coffee cups. The eggnog we found in the fridge. The bottle of whiskey (it was Charley who knew about it) was kept in a cabinet above the sink behind a package of paper plates and some cleaning supplies. The bottle was about half empty when we started drinking. Now it sat on the table next to us, almost spent.

"Well, Leo, that is a personal question, isn't it?"

"You don't have to tell me if it makes you uncomfortable. We can talk about something else. The movie, for example. I don't know why, but I've always found George Bailey to be a particularly relatable character. Thoughts?"

Without getting up, Charley reached over the table and grabbed the whiskey. She added a splash to the eggnog in her cup.

"I met Jerry when I was in college. He worked at this bar everyone went to, and he was the most popular bartender there because he was always so nice and happy all the time. Even when the place was crowded, he had this way of making you feel special. It's hard to explain, but whenever you ordered a drink from him, it felt like that was the only drink he was going to make all night. That's how much he cared."

"So then what? He worked up the courage and asked you out?"

"No," said Charley. "I asked him. I was going through a rough period relationship-wise. Most of the guys I dated I met through the theater department, so a lot of them were either gay or inherently duplicitous."

"Oh."

"Either it was no sex or sex with me but also sex with three other girls at the same time."

"I can see how that wouldn't be ideal."

"I know Jerry isn't the most handsome guy in the world," she said. "Even back then he was overweight. But he loves me, you know. He really loves me. I mean it. He loves me. And I thought—" Here Charley took a long drink from her nog. "I thought he would make a great father one day. He's the kind of guy you want to have kids with."

On the TV, George Baily had just stumbled across his wife to discover that in this parallel, George Baily-less reality, she'd grown up to be a rather stuffy librarian with no time for strange men on the street claiming to be her husband. Charley, meanwhile, had finished her nog and was now pushing things around the fridge in search of another carton. I didn't realize how warm her body was until it wasn't there next to me anymore.

"Do you mind if I ask if you and Jerry are still trying?"

"Off and on. More off than on."

"I'm sorry. I know that can be hard."

"There it is. I knew there was another one in here." She pulled out a fresh carton of eggnog and set it down on the table. "Can I top you off, Leo?"

"Please."

"With whiskey?"

"Is there any other way?"

She smiled at me. She was pretty flushed at this point and all the more beautiful because of it.

"I'm glad you're drinking with me. It's nice that you aren't judgmental about it, which no offense, but I kind of expected, you being a priest and all."

"Let he who is without sin cast the first stone." I downed what was left in my Styrofoam coffee cup.

"You should know I haven't drunk this much since college. I'm a light-weight now. It's already starting to get to me." After settling into the couch, she handed me my cup and then went back to leaning against my side. "When I was a student, I used to keep a tumbler and a bottle of scotch at my desk at all times. I would stay up really late at night, drinking and writing plays because all the great writers I knew were alcoholics."

"Do you still write?" I asked her. "I would love to read your work. Jerry's told me it's quite good."

"Ha!" Charley took another drink of nog. She was developing a mustache of sorts. "My husband's sweet but he knows nothing about drama. All my plays are garbage."

"I'm sure that's not true. If you're comfortable sharing them…"

She turned to look at me. She was sitting on the couch between me and the window, and it just so happened that from my perspective, her head was perfectly framed within a square

44

of falling snow. "You want to hear something that's absolutely going to break your heart?"

I told her no, but to go ahead and say it anyway.

"I don't like to admit it, but if I'm being honest with myself, I think one of the big reasons I want to have children so bad is because I've utterly failed as a playwright. It all has to do with my creative urge. I have this desire inside me to make something beautiful, something good and pure and lovely, something beyond myself. I used to think it would be the next great American play, and then when I married my husband, I thought it would be a little girl or boy, but now…well, now I just don't know." She shook her head and took another drink. "Anyway, you must think I'm pretty selfish, huh?"

I told her no, I didn't think that at all.

"Here you are, a man who's dedicated his entire life to serving those less fortunate, listening to a woman bitch about not having kids or a hit play. It's disgusting how I indulge my unhappiness. I know there are people in this world with real problems, like children starving to death on the streets, or women beaten to an inch of their lives by men who claim to love them. But why am I telling you? You must have seen all that and worse at St. Raphael's."

"Sure," I said, "but just because people are living in poverty, that doesn't make them miserable."

"You aren't happy here either, are you, Leo?"

I didn't answer.

"I've known you for a long time now. I can tell you'd rather be someplace else."

I still didn't answer. I looked away and noticed that the picture on the TV was starting to get fuzzy, as if the snow from outside had somehow drifted into the machine, disrupting whatever divinely-prescribed, life-altering lesson George Bailey was supposed to be learning. When I turned back to

Charley, she was even closer to me than before. She put her hand against my cheek.

"Leo?"

I didn't do or say anything.

"Leo?"

8

"First of all, I just want to say that Jerry was my friend. My best friend. Probably my *only* friend. Even though I hated him half the time and thought he was generally an idiot, I won't deny that he was ten times the man I'll ever be, and it breaks my heart to know he's gone now. When I think about—"

"This is God punishing us," interrupted Charley.

I stared at her, shaken by the blunt, even-toned force of her words. We were standing outside in the cold in the parking lot behind O'Brian's Funeral Parlor. Charley was in her black mourning dress, and I was in my clerics. She wasn't looking at me so much as staring at the space my body occupied. It was obvious Jerry's death had changed things between us, and not in a convenient well-now-that-the-husband's-out-of-the-picture-we-can-finally-run-off-together-and-be-happy kind of way. Charley was shaking because of the cold, but wouldn't let me hold her to warm her up. When she spoke, her words came out in foggy white bursts like the breath of an angry steam engine.

"We've been terrible people. We ran around behind Jerry's back for three years, and now God's punishing us for what we did."

I told her that didn't make a whole lot of sense, considering her husband was the one in the coffin. She slapped me, like really hard. I guess I deserved that. Anyway, maybe she was right since God does have a funny way of dolling out punishment, like when he slaughtered all the first-borns in Egypt, or when he turned Lot's wife into a pillar of salt, or when he put Job through the ringer for, you know, no reason.

"I read the essay," she said.

That was worse than the slap.

"Three Cheers for Pontius Pilate? Are you fucking kidding me? How do you think that made me feel? Have I really made your life so miserable you'd like nothing better than the pleasure of killing God?"

"But that isn't it at all," I told her. "You're the only person I can still cling to. If it weren't for you, if it weren't for what we have—"

"Why did you write it, if not to hurt me?"

I stepped back as if struck. I felt very cold all of a sudden and alone. To Charley's credit, the question of *why* was a fair one, and I didn't have a good answer for her just then. To say that I was unhappy or that I was frustrated…of course I was those things, but it's not like an essay was going to change that. Months earlier, when Fr. Marzano had contacted me with the assignment, I'd agreed to write the article without giving it much thought. The old priest was right about the initial draft. It was a bland and agreeable piece of theology, exactly what the readers of *St. John's Review* had come to expect. But afterwards, the essay left me strangely discomforted. I kept thinking about all the points I'd made regarding sacrifice. Jesus was the Lamb of God, I'd written. His death was foreshadowed in the stories of Abraham and Isaac, Moses and the Exodus from Egypt. By giving up His only begotten son, God had made the ultimate sacrifice in order to restore mankind's relationship with the divine.

But *why*, I wanted to know.

Not, why did God forgive us? I mean, why did it take His only son getting crucified for Him to do it? What was the point? Why not just snap His fingers and—poof—that was it?

After a long silence, Charley reached into her purse and produced a wadded-up tissue, which she used to dry her tears. "Leopold Murphy: a man with absolutely no answers," she laughed coldly.

Turning from her, my gaze fell upon the procession of cars leaving the parking lot. There were no fewer than thirty pairs of taillights floating away in the darkness.

"I never should've stayed that night. I should've walked home in the snow. Even if I'd gotten lost and froze to death, it would've been better to die a faithful woman than watch myself turn into whatever wicked thing I've become. It's funny really. Had you asked me a week ago, I would've told you I didn't deserve my life. I was meant for something bigger, something better. But when I read your essay, it suddenly hit me. If God did come back today, we wouldn't crucify Him. He'd crucify us. People like you and me, we don't deserve better. You understand me, Leo? We've earned our unhappiness."

9

Up in the bell tower, a third of the way through the bottle of whiskey the teachers still kept in in the cabinet behind the cleaning supplies, I wondered to myself whether it would hurt, the fall I mean, if I were throw myself over the ledge and onto Charley's garden. Worst case scenario was a ruptured spine or maybe a broken leg or two or something equally painful and debilitating but also non-lethal. I thought about who would find me come morning now that Jerry was dead. Had the new groundskeeper been hired yet? Probably not. Replacing the pastor was the bigger priority. Plus, Jerry's things were still here. In a little pile in the corner sat his thermos, his scarf, an extra pair of gloves, his Bible. I wasn't drunk enough to envision his ghost coming back to reclaim these items, but I was sufficiently crocked to imagine the objects I myself would leave behind after my death. The list was pathetic and short and not worth recounting. Even more pitiful were the people, or rather *lack* of people, who would miss me. I hadn't lied to Charley before. Jerry Campbell really was my one good friend, and I had no family to speak of except my brother with whom I technically hadn't spoken in years.

A long, fiery swig of whiskey.

I let out a chilly gasp of air.

To tell you the truth, I'd often fantasized about my own death, more so when I was younger, and most so during the six years I spent in Seminary. We were all crazy about death back then. We had this secret club that met every Friday exactly at the stroke of midnight. We would gather under a big willow tree behind the school and read from old medieval manuscripts that recounted all these truly horrific scenes of martyrdom. We referred to ourselves unironically as the Dead Saints Society and would spend hours shooting the shit about just what kinds of awesome ritual execution awaited us on the other side of ordination. Having personally always been a sucker for Liberation Theology, I had what one might call a Latino fetish. My perfect death involved me smuggling food and medicine to a village of poor brown people who were oppressed, in ascending order, by a band of ruthless thugs, their fascist dictator leader, and American President Ronald Reagan, who financed the whole operation for some despicable reason I hadn't yet worked out all the details for.

The climax came when I was finally apprehended and brought before the firing squad to meet my maker. Picture a dusty South American road. Blazing sun. Wilted trees. A little boy leads his burro along the ditch with half a plantain tied to the end of a stick. I'm given a cigarette and blindfold and asked if I have any last words. At this point, the camera cuts to an extreme close up of my chiseled jaw and unflinching eyes. I don't say anything at first. I just stare at the men holding the rifles while a beautiful village woman (voluptuous despite her poverty), weeps loudly on my behalf. Her name is Maria Rodriguez. When the current dictator seized power, her husband was tortured and killed, and she vowed never to love again until the day I arrived and taught her, over the course of 120 minutes, more or less, depending on what the studio decides to cut, that we must all keep our hearts open to the world no matter what pain that might bring us. It's a tough, counter-cultural message for this cynical age we live in, but

51

with the right male lead and some skilled directing, the audience will come to understand that idealism doesn't always equate to naiveté and that words like "truth" and "justice" and "humanity" all still mean something. (I should note that Maria and I have a romantic tryst sometime during the second act, but just as the soft guitar music plays us into the obligatory sex scene, I put a stop to things. I tell Maria that yes, she is beautiful, and yes, I've grown to love her, but I have given my life to God and thus must never know the pleasures of a woman.)

Anyway, there I am standing before the firing squad, staring down at least twenty rifles just waiting to wipe me from the earth. They ask me again if I have any last words, and this time I say yes, so Maria shuts up and gives me a chance to talk. "When I give food to the poor," I tell them, "they call me a saint. When I ask why they are poor, they call me a communist," which maybe the audience will catch the Hélder Câmara shout out, or maybe they'll just think I made that up on my own. In either case, it's a pretty badass way to go. Cut to another close up of my face as one of the goons slides on the blindfold. Cut to Maria, sweat dripping into cleavage, crossing herself and then kissing her rosary like a good Mary-worshipping Catholic. Cut back to the firing squad. This is the critical shot of the whole scene, the entire movie actually. We stare down the rifles from my POV, the sense being that it isn't just Fr. Murphy getting gunned down here but the whole audience along with him. The action turns to super slow motion as the rifles recoil. Plumes of smoke curl up from the ends of the barrels. Only it isn't smoke, but feathers and flapping wings. Twenty white doves fly out of the guns and at the screen. We cut to a medium shot, still in slow motion, and watch as the birds swarm around me. They grab my shirt and hair with their talons. One plucks the blindfold from my eyes. The cigarette falls to the dirt. The doves bear me into the sky like an avian cyclone, and they carry me up, up, up, away from the earth, heavenwards.

Ridiculous, isn't it?

I took one last drink of whiskey and then pushed myself off the ground, staggering over to the ledge where I was met by a rush of cold air. Despite my intoxication, I noticed that the country club golf course appeared very beautiful this evening. The driving range was a peaceful green meadow peppered with balls that from this distance could've been the fluffy white heads of dandelions. The valley was lit under a phalanx of ballpark lights. I could hear the metallic twang of club on ball.

It wouldn't hurt, I decided. I was way up in the air, high enough that once I hit the ground I'd go squash just like a bug on a windshield, which was a far cry from martyrdom, but what could I do about that now? Clearly things hadn't turned out the way I'd envisioned. The life of a priest, well it was meant to be more than this, wasn't it? I was supposed to have helped people. I was supposed to have done good work.

Teetering back from the ledge, I knelt in the corner over Jerry's things. His thermos, scarf, and gloves were of no interest to me, but his Bible…now what was in this book that had bestowed upon my friend such blind optimism?

I opened to the psalms and found one that was marked: "Delight thyself in the Lord, and he shall give thee thine heart's desire."

Yeah right.

I was just about to toss the thing aside when a slip of paper fell from its pages. It was a small, crinkled brochure similar to the one Jerry had shown me earlier. "Paradise Cruise Lines," was written across the top. Under it: "Come sail the *Felicity* to the warm harbors of San Juandigo." There were pictures of the ship, the island, various happy people. "Experience the Beauty of our World," read a string of bolded words. "Learn to Love Life Again," said another.

I set Jerry's Bible aside and held the brochure over the ledge, reading by moonlight. The price for this trip was typed in a small font in the bottom corner on the back. A single ticket cost approximately $10,000.

"Huh," I said.

10

Confession: I have a history of theft.

My high school sweetheart was a girl named Caroline McBride who lived in my neighborhood, attended Sacred Heart Academy for Girls, and practiced ice skating every Saturday morning down at the community rink where it just so happened that my brother Stephen and I also played hockey. My senior year (Stephen's sophomore year), we both made varsity for St. Ignatius. Stephen was a backup defenseman. I was the starting center and led the team in both goals and assists. I should mention that ever since I can remember, my brother and I have been fiercely competitive—as in, to an unhealthy degree—which is why he never cheered or banged his stick against the rail with the rest of the squad when I scored, and which is also why when I saw him flirting with Caroline McBride one morning just as she was leaving the ice, I made it my top priority to steal her.

This wasn't too hard considering I was a senior, a hockey star, and a pretty good-looking guy, while my brother, though wicked smart, was basically a nerd who had regularly wet the bed well past his eleventh birthday. I made my move after practice the Saturday before a big game against St. Dominic's. Caroline, who shared the rink with a couple other skaters in the wee hours of the morning, usually just went home to catch up on some sleep when the hockey players took the ice. Today, though, she'd stuck around to watch us scrimmage, or rather to watch Stephen scrimmage, since he'd finally worked up the courage to French her the previous week, which I guess wasn't as horrible an experience as it sounds because there she was, sitting alone on the bleachers with a windbreaker pulled over her sexy ice-skater's getup, clapping whenever baby bro made a good play.

"Yo, Murphy," said Big Billy Bruiser, an absolute gronk of an individual who manned the responsibility of enforcer for our team. "Who's that hot piece of ass cheering for your little brother?"

We were sitting on the bench between lines, and Big Billy Bruiser, who had his stick propped up in his lap, was staring at Caroline McBride and stroking said stick in a masturbatory fashion.

"Hey, idiot, you want to stop that before Coach sees and makes us skate suicides?"

"What's your problem?"

"The girl's Caroline McBride. Sophomore over at Sacred Heart. She lives a few houses down from us."

Big Billy Bruiser, who had finally caught Caroline's eye, winked at her and then made oral-sex motions with his tongue, which Caroline pretended not to notice.

"Damn, Murphy, for a shit defenseman, your little brother has some serious game. What's his secret? He got a big cock?"

"Not particularly, I don't think."

"Well, it's got to be something, because Sweet Caroline is looking just like an angel up there, and if you tell me Stephen Murphy enjoys the pleasure of boning that heavenly creature without so much as the prerogative that comes with having a big cock, I'm going to lose all faith in the order and justice of the universe."

"Tell me something, Big Billy Bruiser. Where the fuck did you learn a word like 'prerogative?'"

He shrugged.

"Anyway, Stephen won't be enjoying the pleasures of Caroline much longer. I plan on seducing her after practice."

Big Billy Bruiser laughed like a brain-damaged rhinoceros through maybe six teeth if we're being generous.

"Murphy, you are a son of a bitch, you know that?"

Coach blew the whistle, which signaled a line change, so Triple B and I leapt over the rail and onto the ice. Stephen, who would have normally shifted out with the rest of the backups, was playing exceptionally well this morning and was thus given the opportunity to stay in a little while longer to see what he could do against the big boys. This was my chance, and I took it. As soon as the puck was chipped into the zone, I put on the burners and sprinted straight for Stephen. He managed to clear the puck all right, but what he didn't expect was my crosscheck which sent him face first into the boards.

"What the fuck was that?" yelled Coach, slamming his clipboard to the ground.

The trainer hurried out onto the ice to attend to Stephen. Big Billy Bruiser skated up next to me and passed along his compliments via a stiff punch to the shoulder. Caroline McBride, who was now standing on the bleachers trying to get a better view of her bruised and battered beau, had a look on her face like someone had murdered her cat. Stephen hadn't moved since crumpling to the ice. The trainer knelt over him, shaking his head.

"Goddammit, Murphy, you broke your own brother's collarbone."

A couple teammates assisted Stephen back to his feet. He glared at me, obviously hurt, but fighting with all his will not to show it. We both knew there was no physical pain that could compare to the humiliation of admitting defeat. When I told him not to worry, I'd make sure Caroline got home all right, he spat blood on the ice.

57

An hour later, Stephen was still in the locker room getting worked on when I finally completed the suicides Coach had me skate by way of punishment. Instead of going home with the others, Caroline had stayed in the bleachers the whole time, just watching and waiting until Coach finally thought I'd had enough. I fell to the ice and lay there on all fours, trying to catch my breath. When I got up again, Coach was gone and Caroline McBride was standing before me looking like she was about to spit fire.

"How's it going?" I said.

"You're a real piece of shit, you know that?"

This was exactly the kind of take-no-bullshit intensity that made Caroline one of the best junior skaters in the city, not to mention a pretty sexy broad with whom I'd eventually grow quite fond and probably would've dated regardless of my competition with Stephen. She got up really close to me and said, "I thought brothers were supposed to have each other's back."

"Yeah, well, I thought guys weren't supposed to have their girlfriends fight their battles."

I pushed past her and climbed over the rail and onto the bench where I set aside my stick and started unlacing my skates. I didn't give her the satisfaction of looking up, but I could tell I'd really pissed her off.

"I don't know what you see in him anyway. Stephen's not exactly a great catch."

"Oh, right," said Caroline. She climbed over the railing and stood next to me. "I'd be much better off with someone like you, Mr. Fucking Pee-Wee Hockey Star. God, yes, yes, please score another goal. You're making me so wet. If you beat St. Dominic's this week, I'm just going to fucking come."

"You would."

"Excuse me?"

"You would be better off with someone like me."

I stopped unlacing my skates for a second so we could look at each other. Like I said before, I was a pretty handsome guy when I was younger. It looked like Caroline was choking on a pretzel or something.

"You have a lot of nerve, Leopold."

"You can call me Leo."

"Shoving your little brother into the boards like that just so you could—"

"What? Sue me. I'm shy. I didn't know any other way to get you to talk to me." I started unlacing my skates again. "If you want to know the truth, I've been kind of jealous these last couple weeks. I've had a crush on you ever since your family moved into the neighborhood, and then you started going out with my own brother as if to spite me."

"This is so much bullshit it's not even funny."

"So you'll dump Stephen then?"

"I can't believe you have the balls to pull this kind of bullshit stunt."

"And go out with me instead?"

"It infuriating," said Caroline. "This is exactly what's wrong with the world. This is why women have been oppressed for thousands of years. It's because guys like you think that just because you're good-looking, and just because you're some hot-shot varsity hockey player, that automatically means any girl you want will instantly drop her panties the second you ask her to."

Caroline really was sexy when she got fired up like this. I swear, at this point, it was like 30% filial malice, 70% carnal desire.

"So then your answer is…?"

She glared for about thirty seconds without saying a word. Then: "Stephen's not my 'boyfriend' per se. We just made out once."

"I really do like you, Caroline."

"Leo, goddammit, this is so fucking wrong."

11

"Oh, yes, this is right. This is so, so right. Yes, right there. That's the spot. Your hands are magic. Don't stop. Keep going. If I moan too loud, just shove a pillow in my mouth."

The masseuse smiled bashfully as she adjusted the umbrella against the Caribbean sun.

"Why did you stop?" Laurie Hamilton asked her.

"I believe you're making the priest uncomfortable."

"What? Is this true? Am I making you blush, Fr. Murphy?"

I let out an involuntary whelp—the sound a small dog makes when it gets its tail stepped on—as Ivan Drago, or whatever his name was, pulverized my rhomboids, major and minor, with his deadly Soviet mitts.

"Too hard?"

"Yes, too hard!" I said.

"No, too *tight*," said Drago. "Back is like foreshank of cow. Good for nothing but stew."

Laurie, who was entirely loosened up via her third daiquiri of the afternoon, started laughing atop the table next to me. "And my friends tell me I'm stressed. They haven't seen stress. Fr. Leo Murphy: stress personified." She flipped the page of her romance novel. "You know what you should do, Hans? Run down below deck and get one of those mallets they use for tenderizing steaks."

Instead he re-lathered his death clamps with a squirt of coconut oil and resumed my torture.

"I'm glad you're—ah!—finally enjoying yourself, Ms. Hamilton, albeit at the expense—ow!—of my spine."

Laurie turned her head. "What can I say? I enjoy watching men squirm."

This made a lot of sense, professionally speaking. Back in the real world, Laurie Hamilton was Laurie Hamilton, J.D. of Hamilton and Veatch, a swanky, all-female law firm that specialized in ruthless divorce settlements. "An office of pants-suited Amazons," is how she described the place. After big cases, they would all gather to celebrate at this particular Brazilian restaurant where servers made the rounds bearing machetes and skewers of roasted meat. Laurie was fifty-five years old and recently divorced. The point of this cruise—it was her co-workers who organized the thing—was to forget all about her ex-husband's "emotional neediness" and instead find some young tropical hunk with one of those V-shaped pelvic muscles. Classic *How Stella Got Her Groove Back* situation.

"What's that you're reading?" I asked her.

"Oh, this?" She handed over the romance novel. "Just some piece of trash the girls picked up for me at the airport. It's supposed to get me in the mood."

There was a dreamy-looking man on the cover holding a broadsword in one hand and a shield with a red cross in the other. Despite being heavily armored, he was also managing to show plenty of skin, for his chain-mail had been slashed open at the shoulder, revealing a sweaty, sculpted bicep and a throbbing pectoral.

"*The Thousand and One Letters of Henry Lancaster*. Is it any good?"

"Oh, God no," said Laurie. "I mean, it could be. There's tons of potential. It's about Henry V and the Hundred Years' War. At the beginning, Henry marries this sexy tavern wench,

Margaret Stonebrook, but he has to keep the whole thing a secret because later he'll need to wed Catherine of Valois."

"Interesting," I said.

"Not really," said Laurie. "They completely gloss over 15th century marriage law, not to mention Franco-Anglo relations. Meanwhile, an entire chapter is dedicated to describing the king's scepter."

I flipped to a page at random:

My Dearest Margot,

It is done. Agincourt is ours at last. I cannot tell thee how oft I thought of you upon those ramparts. With blood and fire all around, it was God's grace and your prayers—these two things alone—that kept me safe. Now it is over, and there is much rejoicing in our camp. Yet, wherefore art this hole in mine heart, dearest love? It is thine eyes I miss. And thine touch. Oh, thine touch. I quiver at the imagining. Dost thou quiver also? Think of me and quiver, fire of my life, that we may be bonded o'er all these leagues of suffering.

"See what I mean?" said Laurie.

"I see what you mean," I told her. "There's a lot of quivering. Is the whole book written in letters?"

"Uh-huh, it's one of those, what do you call them, epistolary novels? It's actually a best-seller according to my associates, so I guess I hold the minority opinion."

"Best-seller, huh?" I reexamined the jacket cover while Ivan Drago went to work on my latissimus dorsi. The guy they got to pose for Henry must've spent like sixteen hours a day waxing his chest and doing upper-body lifts. "In your opinion, Ms. Hamilton, are women naturally drawn to the epistolary form?"

"You're asking me to speak for my entire sex?"

"I'm just looking for some sound counsel on the matter."

Laurie shrugged and sucked down her daiquiri until there was nothing left but the ice.

62

"I don't know, Fr. Murphy. I think most everybody appreciates a good love letter, don't you think?"

"Yeah," I said. "I think you're right."

12

Dear Charley,

I've been deliberating on the question all day, and I've finally decided that I may as well continue writing you these emails whether you answer them or not. What prompted this conclusion? Well, it's a funny thing really. You'll laugh when you hear it. You see, the whole process reminds me of prayer. Here I am, floating somewhere in the Caribbean, laying bare my soul via international post, and meanwhile you're back in Chippewa County, providing no response whatsoever. It's like that moment right before sleep when you talk to the dark space above your bed as if it were an invisible and benevolent intelligence that gives two shits about your problems. I'm kidding, of course. I've seen and touched you on numerous occasions, sometimes even intimately. Still, it'd be nice to receive some word just to remind me that I'm not writing into the void here. I trust you've received my previous (what is it now?) *eight* attempts at correspondence. If not, allow me to summarize: I've decided to take a long overdue vacation. Notice I say "overdue" and not "well-deserved," for you're right, I've been a terrible person lately. Angry, inconsiderate, solipsistic. I won't deny the charges. Call me an adulterer and a dirty thief on top of it. For a long time now, I've held a strong distaste for the whole of creation, and that includes myself.

Oh but I do so desperately wish to be different!

That's the entire point of this cruise: to learn how to be happy again. I believe that if I'm to accomplish this anywhere, it'll be here, aboard the *Felicity* (or else later at the resort in San Juandigo), for I've been consistently reminded that Paradise Cruise Lines makes it their business to turn people happy. Why just the other day, I was sitting poolside on the top deck of the ship, sipping rum and mango juice, listening to the waves flow by. I was perfectly content by all physical metrics. My belly was filled with prime rib and lobster. My muscles were loose and tingling via a mid-afternoon massage. The Caribbean sun was a warm blanket lain over me. And yet even in the midst of all these comforts, I discovered that somehow a frown had settled upon my face, or rather, I didn't discover it myself, but was informed of it by a passing Luxury Consultant. (You remember how they call everyone aboard the ship either "guest" or "Luxury Consultant" as if the words "customer" and "employee" were the deadliest of taboo?) Well, this particular Luxury Consultant—he was a younger fellow, fair-haired and chipper, small, exhibiting the kinetic energy of a hummingbird—this particular LC hovered over to my chair wearing a grave expression. "Sir," he whispered, "is something the matter?" "Why do you ask?" I inquired. "Well…it's just…" He leaned in close and, still speaking in a hushed tone as if his very words could spark a panic amongst the other guests, reported that I appeared dissatisfied for some reason and that I should please tell him the cause of my displeasure so that he might immediately dispel it.

I must admit, this came as something of a shock, for I didn't *feel* displeased at all. At least I didn't think I did. Don't get me wrong, there were many things to be upset about: Jerry's death, my defrocking, the sorry state of our relationship. But if I'm to be honest with you, I wasn't thinking of any of that when the LC fluttered by. I wasn't thinking anything at all really. I was simply vegetating, floating along in my default state of existence, completely oblivious to the fact that something inside me has been tragically miscalibrated.

I mean are other people just naturally more inclined to happiness than me?

This is a strange and horrifying prospect and would be cruelly unfair if true. Honestly, what kind of God would allow such discrepancies? In my opinion, there are certain attributes like height and the ability to throw a football, where inequality is permissible, but other things (the capacity for happiness chief among them) must be equally distributed. Clearly this is not the case, though, for even here, in the lap of luxury, catered to by myriad indulgences, a frown appeared upon my face. More frightening yet, I was unaware of the frown's existence until notified of it.

"Sir?" said the Luxury Consultant, backing away as if from a leper. "Sir, is there anything I can do for?"

I wanted to tell him yes, there was. Open me up and fix my broken parts. Everyone else here seems to be enjoying himself. Allow me to experience some of that same feeling.

Instead I just smiled at the man—one of those forced smiles in which only the lips move and the eyes don't change at all—and ordered another rum and mango juice, which he brought out right away.

I tell you all this, Charley, not to illicit your sympathy, but to give you some small hope for the future. You see, I don't want to be the way I am. I want to be better, happier, more alive. I want my default adjusted, so to speak. Perhaps this vacation will teach me a thing or two about accomplishing this. Would you like it if I returned to you a changed man? Maybe then you would love me as I love you, and together we could make a fresh start of things. Anyway, I'll continue to write you whether you answer or not, though in all honesty, I do hope you reply.

Affectionately yours,
Leo

13

I was walking back to my room from the *Felicity's*
computer lab when I noticed that the boy at the bar in the
magician's costume was the first sad-looking person I'd seen
in three and a half weeks. He was also enormous: close to
seven feet tall and with shoulders so wide his crimson and
black cape looked more like a theater curtain than an article of
clothing. He was sitting alone, nursing a screwdriver. Every
few sips, he would cough violently and make a disgusted face,
but then he would straighten himself out again and continue
drinking. I discovered, as I sat down next to him, that the
sleeve of his right arm was blackened and smelled vaguely
smoky as if recently set aflame. His top hat was likewise
charred. It balanced atop his head, slightly askew, and
intermittently, playing cards would topple from it.

"First screwdriver?" I asked him.

"How could you tell?"

"You're drinking it like medicine. How old are you
anyway?"

"Eighteen."

"Then let me buy you beer. You'll like it better. Not as
much Vitamin-C, but when you puke, it won't come out all
pulpy."

I hailed the bartender and ordered us a couple of cold ones. After introducing myself, the kid told me his name was Tobit Portnoy and that he was the *Felicity's* magician if I hadn't already put that together. Rather, he *had been* the magician up until about an hour ago, which is when he'd gone and gotten himself fired.

"Fired? No kidding?"

"No kidding, Fr. Murphy. And I mean that in both senses of the word." He held up the burnt end of his sleeve as evidence.

It was his assistant's fault primarily. The girl they'd stuck him with, she wasn't his normal girl. She didn't know how to handle the lighter fluid in the right way, and so when they came to the big finale, Dante's Ninth Circle or whatever, the flaming ring that was only supposed to rotate around the stage like an incendiary hula hoop actually broke its orbit and went flying into the audience. Fortuitously, there were no fatalities, though one woman had her blouse scorched off while another collapsed due to stress. Worst of all was the Vietnam vet who flashed back to his glory days of Napalm and Agent Orange and started screaming his head off for everyone to get down and watch out for Charley.

"Long story short, I'm pretty sure that was my last show for a while," said Tobit. He took a long, sad drink from his beer, which he then thanked me for, because I was right, it was a great deal more palatable than his screwdriver.

"What happened to her?" I asked.

"Who?"

"Your normal girl. You said they stuck you with somebody new?"

This must've been a delicate topic, for no sooner had the words left my mouth than Tobit stiffened and turned quiet.

"Do you want another one of those?"

"I shouldn't drink too much. I'm unemployed."

"Nonsense. Unemployment is a perfect reason to drink. It's right up there with peer pressure and to kill feelings."

He gave me a curious look and asked, "What kind of priest are you, anyway?"

"Technically I'm not."

"Pardon?"

"Not a priest, I mean. I've been I've been kicked out, disqualified, sent to the principal's office and then expelled. What you have to understand is that God and I haven't been on the best terms of late. We have our differences, He and I. For example, I don't like how He spends all His time allowing holocausts to happen and not talking back when I pray. He, in turn, probably doesn't appreciate that I...well, we don't need to get into the specifics just now."

Tobit took another drink from his beer. He stared at me for a long while without saying a word. Finally: "What did you do?"

"To get defrocked?"

He nodded.

"Tell you what," I said. "Let's hear your story first. After that, I'll answer any question you've got."

14

Tobit Archibald Portnoy, aka Allejandro the Magnificent, was the third and largest son of southern Missouri cattle ranchers Sherwood and Ruth. From the day he was born, one could tell Tobit was "different." Because he was so big (even as an infant), a cesarean was required to deliver him. Upon exiting his mother's womb, Tobit did not scream or cry or make any sound at all. In fact, when the doctor pinched him, he merely turned his globular head and frowned, as if to say, "Why would you pinch me, doctor? What have I ever done to you?"

"What a curious boy! He's by far the largest child I've ever delivered, and yet he makes not a peep. Do you mind if I take a picture of him for the paper?"

Since Ruth was still loopy via the anesthetics, the question was posed to Sherwood, the infant's father, who, hailing from a long line of cattle ranchers, found nothing odd in documenting a prodigious birth. He agreed to the photographing immediately, and so with Amos and little Eli put in for scale (these were Tobit's two older brothers), the picture was snapped, sent, and published in the *Mount Sinai Herald* under the headline, "Big Baby Breaks Records at 16 lbs. 4 oz. Mother Recovering."

The Portnoys became minor celebrities because of Tobit. Not long after the story broke, neighbors from as far away as Cobalt and Huffington, MO began arriving at the ranch hoping to catch a glimpse of the enormous child. The visitors were met with a mix of bashfulness and good will. Ruth offered fresh lemonade and squares of leftover casserole to anyone who was hungry, while her husband, a rather stiff and unwelcoming man by nature, said things like, "Yep, he sure is a big one" and "Nope, there's no telling where he got it from." It was Amos and Eli, nine and six years old, respectively, who really got a kick out of all the attention. When their parents weren't looking, they'd heft baby Tobit out of his crib and put him on the back of Duke, the family dog, or if their fans wanted something more daring, they'd fill a laundry basket full of pillows and blankets, strap a pee-wee football helmet onto their younger brother, and send him careening down the basement stairs like a bobsledder.

Their most daring stunt was inspired by a local Channel 5 newsman who had referred to Tobit as "little Paul Bunyan." Under the cover of darkness, Amos and Eli stole a pair of brushes and a bucket of blue paint from the toolshed and then snuck into the birthing stable where a cow had just calved the previous week. The next morning, when their mother was out on the porch showing off the baby to a family from Cicero, the brothers led a bright blue calf into the yard, proclaiming, "Meet Babe the Blue Ox!" The visitors all laughed and snapped pictures and eventually goaded Ruth into holding Tobit up next to the animal, because wouldn't you know it, he just so happened to be wearing a red and green flannel lumberjack onesy that morning, and if he had only had a little ax to hold, it would've been the most adorable thing anyone had ever seen.

Sherwood watched all this happen through the kitchen window while eating his morning slice of dry toast and drinking his morning cup of black coffee. He was a simple, God-fearing man who loved his family, his cattle, and his country, and didn't much care for things like Democrats or nonsense. In his opinion, this nonsense with Tobit had gone on just about long enough. Later that night, after Babe the Blue Ox had unfortunately died of fume-poisoning, he removed his belt and whipped his two eldest sons while reading aloud select passages from *Leviticus*. Then, when punishment had been meted, he announced to the family that they would be welcoming no more visitors from now on. Tobit was a boy, he said, a child of God, and not some circus-freak to be gawked at. It was about time they all started treating him like a member of the family.

15

Fifteen years later, Tobit was 6 feet 8 inches tall, weighed 350 lbs., and could throw a barrel of corn-feed clean over the barn without so much as grunting. He was also a freshman at Mount Sinai Southern Baptist High School where his older brothers had played football in their tenure (QB and middle linebacker, respectively) en route to winning five state championships between them and becoming all-around MSSB legends. Coach Moses (real name) nearly ejaculated in the crotch of his khaki shorts the first time he saw Tobit in person. He'd heard rumors of the boy, vaguely recalled the story of his birth in the *Mount Sinai Herald*, but never in his wildest wet dream had he ever imagined a kid so perfectly built to play left tackle.

"Son, I ain't gonna lie to you," he said to Tobit after pulling him out of first period Algebra to take him down to the coach's office where they sat on a dingy, mildew-smelling couch, eating donuts, and watching old game footage of Amos and Eli Portnoy. "You are the biggest, strongest, scariest motherfucker I've ever seen walk down the halls of this school. Your brothers were great football players when they played for me, but I have a feeling they ain't nothing compared to you. I can't stress enough how much I want you to strap on some pads and knock helmets for us. I want it so bad I would kill somebody, or even get down on my knees and pray. I would literally part the Red Sea to get you to anchor our offensive line."

This was something Coach Moses said a lot, as in "I would literally part the Red Sea to get out of this ticket, officer," or, "I would literally part the Red Sea to get you to blow me, baby." One could just tell he thought it tremendously clever.

"Well, son, what'll it be?" said Coach. "All the D-linemen in the state are shaking in their panties waiting for your answer."

Tobit did not play football for Mount Sinai Southern Baptist High School. Despite his gargantuan mass and Herculean strength (the kid really was built to pancake pass rushers), he had no interest in the game outside a mild curiosity regarding its complicated rulebook. This had less to do with an aversion to *physical* violence as it did an obsession with *imagined* violence, and by that I mean Tobit had become extremely invested in the fantasy role-playing game, *Dungeons and Dragons*, which if you are unfamiliar, usually involves a group of nerdy friends sitting around someone's basement, rolling dice and pretending to slay hill giants. Tobit started playing *D&D* when he was in middle school. By the time he arrived at MSSB, he was quite expert. When he wasn't serving as dungeon master, he assumed the role of Obglor son of Hobglor, a level 35 dwarf wizard (lawful good), with a mean Cone of Cold and surprisingly high charisma. Tobit had to keep all this secret from his parents because Sherwood and Ruth considered *Dungeons and Dragons* to be a form of Satanic worship, so *D&D* nights were mostly held at the house of Madonna Garfield, a very pale and very skinny girl who worked part time in the kitchen of Mount Sinai's Alamo Steakhouse.

Obviously Tobit had a major crush on Madonna. She was smart and deep and beautiful and misunderstood by everyone except him. She wore jet black nail polish and purple lipstick

74

and was so white people wondered if she had a Vitamin D deficiency. Her parents, who were Catholic, sent her to Mount Sinai Sacred Heart instead of Mount Sinai Southern Baptist, but despite being Catholic, they'd named her after Madonna the pop-star and not Madonna the mother of God. Madonna took offense to this. When she spoke of her parents (which wasn't often), she spoke wickedly. She said things like, "Daddy does a thousand push-ups a day to forget how sad he is" and "Mommy fakes 90% of her orgasms." Madonna's plan was to save up enough money to buy a car and then drive to New York where she would start a kick-ass feminist punk band which would also solve rape and homicide cold cases when they weren't busy playing gigs. Punk music was the only type of music Madonna could stomach. She hated all other music, though she hated pop music especially, and out of pop music, she hated Madonna's pop music most especially. When playing *Dungeons and Dragons*, Madonna would sometimes cast a Cone of Silence spell for no reason in particular. (Tobit found this wildly attractive, though he couldn't say why.) Her character was Bethezda, Princess of Screams, a level 28 half elf half goblin who was technically chaotic evil but still associated with Tobit's Obglor son of Hobglor along with the other more ethically centrist members of the party. On rare occasions, Madonna would play with her backup character, Gwendolen, a level 3 forest nymph with an ability called "unearthly beauty." Gwendolen would always die early in the adventure, and usually in some rather nasty manner such as incineration via fireball or getting herself skewered at the end of a Bugbear's spear. This never seemed to bother Madonna much.

The best night of Tobit's life, according to Tobit, was a late-summer evening right before the start of freshman year when he and his buddies snuck over to Madonna Garfield's place to play some *D&D*. His buddies were these really geeky kids with your standard back and face acne and lack of social skills that accompanies a certain genre of adolescence. They gravitated to Tobit because they shared similar interests vis-à-vis the fantasy nerd sub-culture and also because by hanging around Tobit they were ensured complete immunity from bullying. For some complicated set of circumstances that I won't get into here, these buddies had to peace out early on the night in question, leaving Tobit and Madonna alone in the Garfield's basement sans parental supervision. You can see where this is headed. In regards to sexual experience, Tobit was like a level 2 or 3, meaning that while he hadn't technically kissed a girl, he had seen plenty of naked girls via the old Playboys bequeathed by brother Amos. Tobit had masturbated a lot, for which he felt horribly guilty, not that it stopped him. He had also boned-up on the how-to articles and was fairly certain he could perform the sensitive feat of cunnilingus if the situation required. Some girls liked it, some didn't, he knew.

As for Madonna, Tobit imagined her as more of a level 16 or 17, which turned out to be completely false, though such mistakes are often made in regards to dark, counter-cultural chicks who give off airs of jaded promiscuity. Madonna, however, was far from promiscuous. In fact, she was a virgin (not even oral or any finger business) and had decided to follow the letter of the law regarding her catechism and reserve intercourse for the sacramentally-graced context of marriage. (This was another indirect jab at her parents, who like most Catholics, had indulged in pleasures of the flesh pre-nuptially.) For all her punk music and black nail polish, Madonna was just as nervous and awkward as Tobit was about finding themselves alone together in her basement. She, too, had never been kissed. She, too, wouldn't totally hate trying it.

She said, "Hey, TP, How come your folks don't like you playing *D&D*?"

"Religious reasons."

"Is having fun against your religion?"

76

"More or less."

"But really?"

"It's an injunction against witchcraft. My parents think playing *Dungeons and Dragons* is like performing witchcraft."

Madonna laughed. "Oh, you're serious?"

"They burned all my *Harry Potter* books when they found them under my bed."

"Gee, that's rough, though to be fair to Ruth and Sherwood, the series really does fall off after *The Goblet of Fire*."

Tobit was so happy they were talking he didn't even argue this point.

Madonna said, "So what's the deal with this witchcraft thing? Is it like any hint of magic is automatically the work of Satan?"

"Pretty much."

"So...palm readings?"

"Yep."

"Tea leaves?"

"Uh-huh."

"Newt's eye? Ouija boards?"

"The tools of Lucifer, Prince of the Damned."

Madonna laughed again. She kicked off her shoes and sat down beside Tobit on the carpeted floor. They were both leaning up against the couch, their feet splayed out under the coffee table. The Garfield's had a pretty sweet basement when it came to hanging out. It helped that neither of Madonna's parents spent much time down here. Her father participated in triathlons and insisted there was mold in the walls that messed with his lungs, while her mother, a former Miss Missouri Beauty Queen, passed most of her days in the upstairs living room watching soap operas and drinking Bloody Mary's. Tobit was confident that any move to be made stood like a zero percent chance of being thwarted via parental interference, which of course didn't make it any easier to actually make that move.

"What about card tricks?" said Madonna.

"Sorry?"

"Card tricks. You know, 'pick a card, any card.' Where do Ruth and Sherwood come down on card tricks?"

"I don't think that kind of thing is technically magic."

"Well, yeah, but neither is *D&D, technically.*"

Tobit shrugged. At this point, most of his mental energy was going into controlling basic and potentially-embarrassing body functions such as sweating and farting. He wasn't really too concerned about the intricacies of his family's moral code.

"I love a good card trick. And pulling bunnies out of hats. And cutting people in half, only not really. God I eat that shit up."

"Are you being serious right now?"

"The sexy thing about magicians is that they're basically the ultimate nonconformists. Just think about it. While anarchist punk rockers rebel against an arbitrary and oppressive *political* reality, magicians rebel against an arbitrary and oppressive *physical* reality. They really turn it up to 11, don't you think?"

"We're talking about those guys who perform at children's birthday parties?"

Madonna looked Tobit straight in the eyes. There was an expressionlessness to her face that was simultaneously beautiful and terrifying. Like a black hole: the opposite of emptiness often mistaken for emptiness. She said, "I think it's really admirable how you sneak over here and play *Dungeons and Dragons* even though Sherwood would probably tan your hide if he ever found out. You're really brave to do that, TP. I'm really impressed by your bravery."

Tobit was doing some serious perspiring at this point. He said thanks but that it was no big deal really.

"You know, I'm not technically supposed to be down here alone with boys."

"Uh-huh."

"The parental units are insuring themselves against teenage pregnancy, the worst type of pregnancy."

"Should I…?"

"Do whatever you want. I'm just giving you all the facts."

Tobit could barely look at Madonna now. He was so nervous his hands were trembling. He could literally feel his heart shaking inside his chest. He knew what his next move should be—either the suave arm-around-shoulder maneuver or else the hand-to-knee gambit—but the chasm between knowing and doing was near infinite. I'll spare you all the clunky *D&D* metaphors he used to describe the scene (let's just say the terms "blinding beauty" and "paralyzing charm" were thrown around more than necessary) and instead jump ahead to the moment when he finally nutted-up and did it, kissed her, dove straight in, said, "fuck it, spaceship, I'm steering for the abyss."

Don't worry, this isn't going to turn into one of those luridly didactic morality plays about the dangers of premarital-sex. In the nomenclature of baseball, Tobit and Madonna barely rounded first, which was just about far enough in my opinion considering these two lovebirds had only graduated middle school at the time. The point being is that when Coach Moses yanked TP out of first period algebra a few months later to take him down to the film room and ask him to play left tackle, the boy broke his heart not just because of his afterschool *Dungeons and Dragons* obligations but because he also had a real life girlfriend with whom he had developed a brand-new, totally radical, and necessarily hush-hush vocation. By that I mean Tobit had become an amateur magician with Madonna Garfield serving as his assistant.

They practiced in her basement mostly, recreating tricks (rather, *illusions*) from a how-to book purchased via the internet which also came with a bunch of cool goodies such as a magician's wand, top hat, trick cards, one of those brightly-colored handkerchief ropes you see pulled out of one's throat, etc. All the packages were delivered to the Garfield residence since Sherwood and Ruth would've had about twenty aneurisms apiece had they discovered what Tobit was up to. (Plus it was Mr. Garfield's credit card that Madonna had stolen to place said orders.) They performed in front of their *D&D* buddies at first, but after a few months of practicing, considered themselves veteran enough to play larger, more hostile venues, such as local birthday parties and even the Cicero High Fall Talent Show, which was in Cicero, MO about forty highway minutes from Mount Sinai. It was Mrs. Garfield who gave them a ride (and also promised to keep the whole thing secret). She was so happy her little girl was finally "opening up" and "letting out her inner beauty" that she even volunteered to help them with their costumes—a stunning purple dress for Madonna (it matched her lipstick), and a flamboyant cape and top hat for Tobit, who couldn't go by "Tobit" anymore, but needed a proper stage name, something bold and daring, like "Udolpho the Bold" or "Benito the Daring." And so it was that lowly Tobit Portnoy was rechristened "Allejandro the Magnificent," and thanks to the help of Mrs. Garfield, he and Madonna were a big hit at the Cicero High talent show where they took second place overall and actually would've won had an autistic sophomore in a wheelchair not butchered R Kelly's "I Believe I Can Fly" to a standing and teary-eyed ovation.

First place trophies notwithstanding, you can imagine how awesome this whole ride was for Tobit. Not only was he sucking face on like a daily basis with the girl of his dreams, but he also loved performing for its own sake. Onstage, in costume, standing there before sometimes dozens of strangers, he felt special/singled-out for something other than his prodigious size, which honestly he'd grown weary of folks

80

telling him how big he was since it wasn't exactly an accomplishment as far as he was concerned and had in fact been a not insignificant hindrance to scoring chicks. But Madonna, bless her soul, didn't mind that her BF outweighed her by let's say 250 lbs. Whenever he visited her at work, she would sneak him free double-bacon cheese burgers or onion rings or whatever else he was in the mood for. She would also tell him all sorts of personal things about herself in these super-serious conversations they'd have between particularly tender and heartfelt kissing. She referred to these conversations as "getting real," as if the rest of her life were somehow unreal, and had confessed to Tobit her biggest fears (loneliness, being ordinary, jumping banana spiders) as well as her greatest hopes and desires, which it's worth noting that her aforementioned punk-rock-homicide-detective fantasy had been replaced by a completely new dream in which she and Tobit traveled the world performing magic together and also adopting an orphan from each country they visited so that by the end of their journey, they had a whole troupe of ethnically diverse assistants with each one bringing his or her own unique talents/cultural vitality to the group and generally being altogether one big loving family.

16

Three years passed in this way, and then Tobit and Madonna became seniors. This is when the trouble started, and it came from an unlikely source: Madonna's father.

Now Mr. Garfield was willing to let a lot of things slide. He didn't argue with his daughter about her choice of wardrobe or makeup or taste in music or the fact that she spent all her free time hanging around Tobit Portnoy, playing make-believe or whatever. He also didn't care that she didn't care about your conventional senior-year-bucketlisty-type shit, like buying a school ring or dumping a newborn at prom. A year earlier, Mrs. Garfield had just about put an icepick through her aorta when Madonna announced she wasn't going to MSSB's Homecoming, but Mr. Garfield only shrugged, slipped on his Nikes, taped up his nipples, and then embarked on a fifteen mile run, which was often his response when confronted with messy family conflicts. Better to avoid than engage was his motto. Unlike his two older cousins, he'd lived through Vietnam and could now apply its lessons to raising a child, which is why it was surprising that he took such an unprecedentedly hard line in regards to higher education.

"He wants me to be a wildcat. Do you believe that shit? A wildcat."

Tobit didn't know if Madonna meant Kentucky, Kansas State, Arizona, Northwestern, Villanova, Davidson, etc. When he asked her to clarify, she just glared at him over her absurdly thick, still-in-the-shrink-wrap SAT prep book and said, "Does it matter?"

Well, it did matter. It mattered a great deal, at least to Mr. Garfield, and it was Arizona, by the way, his alma mater. Years back, he'd run middle distance for the Cats, competing in events like the 800 and the 1200, and though he was no star athlete compared to some of his more highly-recruited teammates, Mr. Garfield took an intense, almost religious pleasure in the sport. To hear him speak of Tucson just before dawn was to listen to poetry. He loved the dry, hot desert air, the sting of lactic acid in the legs. He was fascinated by the vegetation: everything so prickly, ascetic, beautiful. He believed—perhaps not *so* ridiculously—that Madonna would benefit from a place like this. There was no arguing the girl could use more sunlight, and maybe the sun would bring about other changes, too, like frequent smiling or experimentation with more appropriate shades of eyeliner.

"It's crazy, TP. They want me to go into the desert and come out an entirely new person. They're treating me like a drug addict who needs rehab. I feel like a dirty pot waiting to be scoured clean with sand."

Clearly Madonna didn't hold UA in the same high regard as her father. The way she saw it, the school attracted exactly two types of students: your standard rapey fraternity guys and the girls they preyed on: bleached-blonde, orange-skinned, all of them majoring in something easy and probably made-up like sociology. Needless to say, these were not the people with whom Madonna willingly associated, and so she set about sabotaging Mr. Garfield's plans, first by intentionally bombing the SAT and then by tanking as many of her senior year classes as she could manage. Then, later, when the Arizona application arrived in the mail, she took things a step further. They asked for 500 words describing, "what a successful UA freshman looks like to you," and in response, Madonna attached a fifteen page story about a young woman who was murdered by her RA and then fed to actual wildcats kept hidden under the football field. She was fairly confident the piece would trigger about a million red flags for whatever low-level admissions officer was slogging through all these essays, meaning that if her sucky SAT scores and shitty grades didn't keep her out, surely the threat of psychosis would.

Which was great, you know. It was perfectly alright not to go to college. Madonna was pulling in good money from the Alamo Steakhouse, and she and Tobit were getting better and better at their magic. They'd started off playing birthday parties and talent shows, but now, after three plus years of experience, they were regularly booking gigs that actually paid. Soon graduation would come, and the two would set off on the road together, wowing audiences across the country. At least this was the plan.

17

That April, Sherwood Portnoy was showing a cow named Jayne Mansfield at the Butler Country Fair so as to qualify her for state competition. Sherwood loved Jayne Mansfield. He adored her. She was a thirteen-month-old, eleven hundred pound, golden-haired heifer, who happened to possess the long body and perfectly-proportioned rump needed to procure a blue ribbon. In the weeks leading up to the fair, Sherwood visited her stall at least twelve times a day. He bathed her, blanketed her, brushed her gorgeous blonde hair, clipped her hooves, fed her only the choicest grains in carefully-formulated and time-honored proportions. Once, when his wife Ruth came into the barn asking him to sample a variation on her famous Brown Betty, he turned to her sharply and said, "Woman, your cobbler is the last thing on my mind right now."

While Sherwood was busy prepping Jayne Mansfield, Tobit and Madonna were busy practicing their magic. Like Sherwood, they, too, had an engagement at the Butler County Fair. They'd been invited to perform on the main stage for three consecutive days, which was risky business, considering their act was still technically a secret, but when the entertainment manager called offering a whopping $250 per show, they decided it was a risk worth taking.

This was a mistake.

On the last day of the fair, Sherwood was so thoroughly pleased with the frilly purple best-in-show ribbon he'd earned via Jayne Mansfield that he did something entirely out of character. Usually after a competition like this, he'd pack up his trailer and head home to prepare for state, but today he decided to enjoy himself. From a nearby stand, he purchased a funnel cake and a strong cup of coffee, and then he wandered around the fairgrounds, sipping and nibbling, soaking up the bright Missouri sun, breathing deeply the rich stench of cow manure. When he came upon the main stage, he expected to hear fiddling or maybe some banjo music. Instead he discovered Tobit holding a broadsword high above his head about to sever a boxed-in Madonna.

The coffee and funnel cake hit the ground at precisely the same moment.

Then came the anger, bubbling and hot. It was a righteous, Old Testament kind of rage, the type of wrath that smites evildoers and levels cities. To see his own flesh and blood worshipping Satan with that succubus Garfield girl! Sherwood hadn't been this upset since the Carter administration.

"Thou shalt not suffer a witch to live," he prophesied.

The whole crowd turned to look at him.

"A man or woman that is a wizard shall surely be put to death. You shall stone them. Their blood shall be upon them."

You can imagine how messy the situation got. Not only was their act ruined, but Tobit and Madonna had to flee the stage before Sherwood did them bodily harm.

Later, at the Portnoy ranch, after a severe whipping and many *Leviticus* verses, Tobit was forbidden from ever seeing his girlfriend again. Naturally, he snuck out the following evening to meet her at the Alamo Steakhouse. All night, according to the manager, customers had been complaining about overcooked burgers, and it was easy to see why. When Tobit found Madonna in the kitchen, she was standing over a grill of charred hockey pucks, taking an intense, vindictive pleasure in the sizzling of meat.

"I'm not supposed to see you anymore on account of our devil worship."

"We need to get out of here, TP."

"But aren't you working?"

"I mean out of Mount Sinai. The sooner the better. Our parents don't like us, and vice versa. We could leave tonight except neither of us has a car or the money to buy one. How much do you think we could get if we stuck up this joint? Five, six thousand?"

Tobit said he wasn't sure. Anyway, they didn't have guns or ski caps, and it wasn't ethical to go around robbing folks.

"You're right," said Madonna, "but I still think we should leave. Here, I found this the other night. It would solve our transportation issue."

She handed him a job listing for Paradise Cruise Lines. They were looking for a magician and magician's assistant for a nine month assignment aboard the *Felicity*. Pay was competitive and the benefits quite generous.

"This would be a real adventure," he admitted.

"Does that mean you're in?"

Of course Tobit was in. He loved Madonna. He would follow her to the ends of the earth.

"Good. Now I want you to go home and pack your bags. We'll take a bus down to Miami tomorrow night, but before then…" She stared at him over the burning patties. Her eyes narrowed. "Before then, there's one last thing we need to do."

It was a dark, twisted, spiteful plan—like seriously fucked up—and the first step of the operation involved Tobit sneaking into his father's barn at two o'clock in the morning to steal the show cow, Jayne Mansfield. Later that day, the whole Portnoy family packed up and drove to the Alamo Steakhouse for supper, as was their custom on Saturday evenings. Sherwood ordered what he always ordered, the Davy Crockett Burger: a quarter pound of Angus beef loaded with bacon, onion fritters, Colby-jack cheese, etc. A man of few indulgences, he allowed himself an extra side of sweet-potato fries to be shared amongst the table, though a stern look to Tobit made it clear his son's recent transgressions excluded him from the treat. Not that Tobit would've wanted any fries regardless. He'd lost his appetite the moment he saw the entrées come out. Between Sherwood's burger, Ruth's burnt ends, and the mammoth rack of beef ribs split between Amos and Eli, there was enough dead cow here to feed a small village.

"Dear Lord," said Sherwood, "we thank you for this bounty. We ask you to bless our food and our family, especially those who have lately fallen from the path of your righteousness. Strengthen us through this meal that we may follow you in all ways. We ask this in the name of your son, Jesus Christ, Savior of the World, Amen."

"Amen," went the echo around the table.

Tobit remained silent while the rest of the family feasted. Instead of eating, he picked at his loaded baked potato, disgusted with just how much sour cream was piled over the melted cheese.

"What's the matter?" said Amos, looking up suspiciously from his plate.

"Yeah," said Eli. He sucked the last, fatty tendrils of flesh from a rib bone and then popped the thing out of his mouth, holding it like one might hold a cigar. "You ain't touched nothing. Aren't you hungry?"

Ruth glanced up from her platter of burnt ends and frowned.

Sherwood, however, was enjoying his Davy Crockett burger so aggressively that he didn't even notice his son's abstaining. Tobit watched him eat with a mixture of awe and revulsion. He found it incredible that a man normally so reserved could transform before a plate of grilled meat.

Sherwood became something else entirely. All mouth and hunger.

"Eat your potato," said Ruth.

Tobit turned to her, surprised that tears were running down his cheeks.

Her face softened into an expression of confused sympathy. "Look, now he's crying."

"What a baby," said Eli. "Honestly, I'm ashamed to be seen with him."

"This is one of the juiciest, most delicious burgers I've ever had," announced Sherwood from the head of the table. He stuck the last blessed morsel into his mouth and then licked all ten of his greasy fingers. He called over the waiter, Manuel, and asked him to pass along his compliments to the chef. "In fact, bring the guy out here if he doesn't mind. I want to shake this fellow's hand."

Manuel hesitated: "Of course, sir. I'll see what I can do."

Tobit's heart began to pound as he watched the waiter vanish through the swinging doors and into the kitchen.

Ruth asked him what was wrong, why was he trembling?

"Pay attention, all of you," said Sherwood. "Everybody's going to thank this cook when he comes out here. Folks these days think the only people worth celebrating are professional athletes or slutty pop stars, but I tell you, there's dignity in doing good simple work the way it ought be done."

Amos and Eli exchanged a sly grin. Tobit dropped his fork because his hands were shaking so badly. The kitchen doors burst open and out strode Madonna Garfield, pale and skinny, blood up to her elbows, bearing the severed head of Jayne Mansfield.

"Your cow, sir," she said, throwing the head down on the table. It rolled exactly one and a quarter revolutions and then stared up at Sherwood with its fat, bulbous eyes. "I'd thank you for the compliments, but I can't in good faith take all the credit. The beef, you see, was excellent from the start. Some real blue ribbon quality shit."

A stunned silence fell over the table. Then Eli said, "Wow," and Amos said, "Very dark," and Eli said, "Very *Titus Andronicus*, you mean," and Amos said, "Don't be so *udderly* pretentious."

Tobit, meanwhile, had never been more attracted to Madonna than he was in this moment. He didn't know why, but he wanted to throw her down on the table and ravage her right there in front of his whole family, and the only thing that kept him from doing exactly this was the fact that Sherwood was currently retching up his Davy Crockett Burger along with his portion of the sweet potato fries.

The love-making had to wait. Thirty-five minutes to be precise. That's how long it took for Madonna to get fired, for Tobit to be publicly disowned, and for the two blood-splattered lovers to make their escape, sprinting down the streets of Mount Sinai all three and half miles back to the basement of casa Garfield.

"I love you, TP. I love you more than anything. I love you so much it…Christ, I'm out of breath."

Tobit pushed her down on the couch and then planted himself on top of her, tearing off her blouse. Madonna started laughing and then moaned quite loudly. Tobit didn't know what he was doing at this juncture. He was acting on a mix of instincts, personal fantasies, and an anthology of sexual exploits internalized via years of reading Amos and Eli's dirty magazines.

"Jesus, I know I promised myself I'd wait," said Madonna, "but this definitely feels right. Try not to come inside me, though, okay? I don't think we're ready to be parents."

"Sure."

"And I love you."

"I love you, too."

"No, I mean it. I really love you."

90

"I mean it, too."

It was probably for the best that things were interrupted. No sooner had the panties descended to Madonna's ankles, than a soft, inquisitive tapping was heard upon the basement door. It was Mr. and Mrs. Garfield, barging into their daughter's life most inconveniently.

"Hello, honeyboo? Mind if we—oh, hi there, Tobit."

"Good evening, Mrs. Garfield."

He smiled up at her (pillow atop lap) from the end of the couch extremely opposite his girlfriend. They'd just had time to put their clothes back on, though everything was still unbuttoned or inside out.

"Is everything alright down here?" said Mr. Garfield.

"Of course."

"Because it looks like you have blood on your arms."

"Oh, right." Madonna tried to sound as nonchalant as possible. "It's nothing. It's from work."

Her father nodded, not exactly convinced, but willing to let it go as there were more pressing matters to discuss. He stepped forward into the basement, and Tobit noticed he was carrying a large manila envelope.

"This came for you today."

"Yeah?"

"It's from the University of Arizona. Your mother and I wanted to be here when you opened it."

Madonna accepted the envelope in quiet disbelief. Given her grades, SAT scores, and deranged admissions essay, she'd expected a standard rejection letter—a good old "Sorry to inform you..." shoved inside a classic 4x9—but this package was big, thick, heavy. She tore open the seal and pulled out the contents. There was a folder inside bearing the picture of a very diverse set of UA undergraduates studying together in the library.

Mrs. Garfield began to cry softly.

91

Her husband put an arm around her shoulder and said, "Go on. Open it. See what it says."

Tobit watched as Madonna lifted the front flap. There was a handwritten note inside, which she read silently.

"Well?"

"It's from the head of the Creative Writing Department, and also the head of the English Department, and also the chair of the Women and Gender Studies Department. They all read my story."

"What story?" said Mr. Garfield.

Madonna looked up at her parents. She was shaking and maybe even on the verge of tears. "They said they had to pull a bunch of strings because my SAT scores were so abysmal, and my grades didn't help matters either."

"Does that mean…"

"Yes," said Madonna, "yes, they want me. Really, they want me. And they've offered a full scholarship."

It was a shocking development. Mr. and Mrs. Garfield, though somewhat hopeful via the thick envelope, had only expected a conditional acceptance at best, one of those, "you barely squeaked in in here, missy, so don't fuck this up." Now that they knew the truth, a strange mix of pride, relief, and confusion swept over them. They hugged their daughter awkwardly, simultaneously. Madonna wasn't standing, so it ended up being a messy thing: a bunch of grasping limbs and mismatched torsos not accustomed to this degree of proximity. Nevertheless, both mother and father squeezed very tightly upon the flesh they could get to. They were ecstatic, but also quietly ashamed, thinking to themselves, "Who would want our little girl so badly, and why? Is there something obvious we missed about her? We love her, sure, but come on, it's only Madonna."

Neither were literary types, so words like "macabre" and "Kafkaesque" meant nothing to them. They certainly understood "talent," though, and "brave new voice" and "untapped potential" and "genius." Had anyone bothered to ask Tobit, he could've produced a similar list years back, but no one had asked him, and now that the truth was revealed, he wasn't a participant of the celebration so much as a satellite to it, hesitant and self-conscious, like the place kicker on a team that's just won the Super Bowl.

"I'm going to call your grandmother."

"Oh God, she'll be beside herself."

"There're so many things we need to buy."

"A new computer."

"Of course. For her writing."

"Do they say when the semester begins?"

"I'll get the phone. I said I'll get the phone."

While the Garfields ran circles around the basement, Tobit remained on his side of the couch, reading the letter from the three department heads. It had become painfully clear to him that Madonna was no longer his. There were others out there who loved her. He would have to accept that.

"What are you thinking, TP?"

"I guess congratulations."

"Is that it?"

"No."

Madonna wiped some tears from her eyes, which smeared her makeup.

"You aren't coming to Miami, are you?"

She didn't answer.

"I understand that you have to do this."

"You could tell me not to," she said. "Put your foot down and forbid it, and I'll throw away this whole packet, and we can leave for the bus stop tonight."

"I don't think that'd be a good idea."

"No, I guess not."

They stared at each other, not sure what else to say.

Finally: "Will you write me?" asked Tobit.

"Of course," said Madonna. "Every day. You won't even notice I'm gone."

18

The Atlantis Resort Hotel and Casino soared over the western beaches of San Juandigo with all the phallic energy one comes to expect from American architecture. We saw the towers a long way off, hours before docking. Tobit and I were standing along the railing of the *Felicity*'s observation deck, watching the island slowly materialize over the sea. It was bright outside and very hot. The smell of sunscreen was heavy in the air, and an incessant wind blew over the waves and into our faces, seasoning our skin with salt.

"But that's the main thrust of it, isn't it?" Tobit was saying. "Basically, you think I'm an idiot."

"No, not an idiot," I told him. "But people change. Young people especially."

"You haven't even met her, Fr. Murphy. Madonna is different from other girls. We love each other, and nothing's ever going to change that."

"Okay," I said. "I take it back. Basically, I do think you're an idiot. She said she'd write, so where are the letters?"

He gave me a snarky look.

"Listen, we've talking around this point for weeks now. You've shared your story and I've shared mine, and we are irreconcilable in our differences."

Tobit turned back to the sea. "For what it's worth, I think she still loves you."

"Who? Charley?"

He nodded. "I also think you're wrong about Jesus. I wouldn't want to crucify him. I'd want to thank him."

"What the hell do you have to be thankful for?"

"Lots of things. Madonna, for one, my magic, for another."

"Need I remind you that your girlfriend is over three thousand miles from here probably forgetting you ever existed? Furthermore, your magic has gotten you disowned from your family and fired from your job, and what do you have to show for it all except a free trip to a disaster zone?"

Tobit laughed.

"What's so funny?"

"Fr. Murphy, you're being ridiculous. San Juandigo is paradise on earth. Just look at it out there."

I looked, but didn't see anything particularly special.

"The Atlantis Resort: where time stops and luxury begins."

"You stole that from the brochure, and anyway, the hotel and casino might be standing, but the rest of the island has probably gone to shit. There was just an earthquake, remember? Plus, my brother is out there somewhere, most likely adding to the problem."

Tobit just shrugged. "Agree to disagree, I guess."

19

Two hours later, we were sitting next to each other in the hotel shuttle, bouncing east along the dirt road towards the market. After checking into our respective rooms and dropping off our luggage, we'd rendezvoused in the casino lobby where we quickly decided that fresh air and sunlight were preferable to the flashing cacophony of five hundred slot machines. With lunch in mind, we boarded the shuttle and set off for the heart of the island. The drive was pleasant at first. Rolling hills of vegetation opened every so often to reveal a bright blue pond where some of the local children were playing. When the shuttle drove by, they all made faces at us and giggled. One especially daring boy ran up to the side of the road and dropped his pants, though instead of being offended, everyone on the bus was so amused by his pale plump cheeks that we all gave him a strong round of applause, and the driver honked three times in recognition.

Things grew less cheerful, however, the closer we came to the market. The earthquake had toppled many houses here, and the school and the church were reduced to rubble. The people themselves also showed signs of injury. Everywhere I looked, someone was either limping or nursing a broken arm or carrying a child with one leg instead of two. An old man sitting by the side of the road had two craters of scabbed-over skin where his eyes once were.

"The opiate of the masses," I said.

"Huh?" said Tobit.

"It's what Karl Marx called religion. I'm starting to think he wasn't too far off in this regard, because the older I get, the less and less I buy into the whole metaphysical premise of the thing. Angels and demons? Souls? Are we really supposed to believe in this bullshit?"

Tobit gave me a dumbfounded look. "I don't understand. What kind of priest doesn't believe in religion?"

"Well, technically, I'm not really a priest anymore, remember?"

"Sure, but your essay…"

"Three Cheers for Pontius Pilate?"

"Yeah, right, an essay like that suggests a lot of things, but I wouldn't say that atheism is chief among them."

"You're gonna have to explain that one to me."

He shrugged. "I don't know. You seem to be harboring a great deal of resentment towards God. What's the point of all that anger if there isn't a God in the first place?"

Since I didn't have an answer for this, I swiped the brochure from his hands and started reading under the fold entitled, "History of San Juandigo." It was actually some pretty interesting stuff if you could get past the racism. According to the literature, the island was "discovered" during the mid-16th century when a Spanish caravel that was supposed to be headed to Florida got horribly lost, then hit a storm, then capsized, killing every single person aboard save the chaplain, a Jesuit priest named Juandigo. For two days and two nights, Juandigo drifted on the waves, desperately praying the Liturgy of the Hours while clutching to his bookshelf that doubled as a rather effective flotation device. On the third day, weak and dying of thirst, he washed up on shore, where the natives (who had never met a white man) welcomed him with open arms.

They fed the priest, gave him fresh water to drink, and nursed him back to health. As legend had it, Juandigo's recovery was expedited by a certain fruit he'd never seen before. It was big like a watermelon, but pear-shaped, with a thick green husk that you needed a hatchet to cut into, and on the inside, sweet, blood-red flesh. When the priest asked the natives what they called this wondrous delight, they told him a word he later forgot. Instead, he decided to rename it the "Persephone Fruit" after the daughter of Demeter, goddess of harvest. While he was recovering from his shipwreck, Juandigo requested a bowl of Persephone Fruit be brought to his bedside every night. Then, while his healers were asleep, angels of the Lord would come down from the heavens and sit with him, partaking of the delicious fruit. While they ate, the angels informed Juandigo of his new mission, for it was no accident that his ship had capsized.

"You must make Christians of these people," they said. "In the time of Adam, it was acceptable to live as they do, ignorant and peaceful, surviving off the bounty of the earth, but now that sin has entered the world, no man, no matter how remote, is safe. The soul is like ship. It must be kept strong and in good working order. Even the tiniest leaks will prove fatal if left untended."

"Here we are," announced Tobit as the shuttle rolled to a stop.

I handed back the brochure, and we all piled out of the bus and into the market, which was crowded and noisy, one long street of cobblestones with large wooden booths lining each side.

"You there, holy man! You hungry? You want something sweet?" It was a middle-aged woman, dark-complexioned and broad-shouldered, standing behind a booth to the right. "Persephone fruit!" she shouted. "Only five dollars. You won't find a better price."

The produce was hanging in big fishnets on either side of her. She grabbed one and held it up for us. Then she picked up a butcher's cleaver that was dripping with what looked like blood but was actually juice.

"Tell you what, *Padre*. Since you are a man of God, and my son, Bembé, is to be a priest one day, I shall give you this fruit in exchange for only three dollars and a blessing. Bembé, get over here. This man has come to bless you."

Before I could protest, the woman had grabbed her son and was pulling him towards me. The kid couldn't have been a day over sixteen. He wore baggy white trousers and a yellow shirt. His skin was dark like his mother's, but his eyes were brighter and more joyful.

"Peace be with you, *Padre*, and to you, too, sir," he added, bowing to Tobit.

We returned his greeting.

"My name is Bembé Villanueva, and I have recently been filled with the fire of the Holy Spirit. Next year, I will enter the seminary where I will begin my studies in the theology of the Catholic Church. May I ask if you serve in America, *Padre*?"

"Sure," I said. "I used to be the pastor of a church in a place called Chippewa County. You probably don't know of it, but it's near a city called Chicago. Have you heard of Chicago?"

"Oh, yes," said Bembé quite gravely. "*Chicago*. Many are killed there every day. It is a place of horrible violence."

Chop!

I winced as Bembé's mother sliced open the Persephone Fruit. The tough, green husk yielded to her cleaver, revealing insides that were red and gooey.

"When I become a missionary," said Bembé, "I will go to Chicago and bring the word of God to the people."

"Good for you," said Tobit.

I rolled my eyes.

"What's wrong, *Padre*?" asked the boy.

Tobit, Bembé, and Bembé's mother all looked at me. A more gutless man might've been intimidated.

"It's nothing really, but speaking as someone who's actually lived in Chicago, the problems of that city have essentially nothing to do with the word of God. There are bigger issues, you know. Income inequality. Institutional racism. Etc."

Bembé frowned. "*Padre*, I have heard it said that men shoot down other men in the streets. Unless these stories are lies, and I do not believe that they are, then surely these people need to hear the good news of Jesus Christ. For it is written, 'The Lord will judge between nations and settle disputes for many peoples. They will beat their swords into ploughshares and their spears into pruning hooks.'"

"That's all well and good," I replied, "but they don't use swords and spears where I come from. They have guns instead and lots of them."

"What Fr. Murphy is trying to say," said Tobit, "is that the challenges you'll face in America are complex and will require intelligent actions as well as faith. It's like what James says in his epistle: 'As the body apart from the spirit is dead, so faith apart from works is also dead.'"

I gave him a look to let him know that wasn't what I meant at all, and he knew goddamn well it wasn't.

"Of course," said Bembé. "'Let us not love in word or tongue, but in deed and in truth.' Are you a priest as well, sir? Your vestments…I'm not aware of your order."

"Oh no," said Tobit. "These burnt up things are just my magician's costume."

"Brother Portnoy is a Houdini friar," I added.

"Really?" said Bembé. "I've never heard of the Houdinis. When were they founded?"

"Not even a century ago. Have you really never heard of St. Houdini? He was a regular Sebastian when it came to escaping predicaments. They used to chain him to skyscrapers and bury him alive."

"Oh dear," said Bembé.

Tobit frowned and told me that was enough.

"Your lunch, *Padre*," said Bembé's mother, pushing forward the two halves of Persephone Fruit. A sweet, syrupy odor rose from the sweaty flesh.

I thanked the woman and handed over the three dollars.

"And the blessing?"

"Oh, right. I forgot that was part of the deal."

Bembé stood before me, head humbly lowered to receive my blessing. He was so young and stupid, it almost broke my heart to mumble whatever it was I ended up mumbling.

"Thank you, Padre," he said afterwards, grasping my hands tightly. "I won't let you down."

"No, I'm sure you won't."

Tobit wished the boy good luck as we departed. Then, later, while we ate our fruit in the shade of a nearby grove, he said no offense, but I had acted like a real asshole back there in the market, making fun of that poor kid when all he wanted was to do something really selfless and noble.

"What? Are you talking about that Bembé idiot?"

"Yes, of course I'm talking about Bembé," he said, scowling at me over his juicy husk.

I shrugged. "How do you expect me to act when I see a young man so eager to throw his life away?"

"You can't really believe that, Fr. Murphy."

"But I do."

Tobit shook his head and took a couple bites of Persephone Fruit.

"Look," I told him, "I'm not trying to be difficult here, but I have to be honest. Remember, I'm speaking from experience on this matter."

"And what are you saying? That you've completely wasted your life?"

"Well, that's a harsh way to put it, but yeah, more or less."

"I refuse to accept that."

"Whether you accept it or not, it's the way it is."

Tobit was quiet for a long while. As we ate our respective lunches, the only noise that passed between us was the sloshing of juice and sweet flesh. Finally, he looked over and said, "I know you're feeling pretty low right now what with your defrocking and your best friend dying and Charley refusing to run off with you. But I believe things are going to turn around for you, Fr. Murphy, because I have a hunch God put you on this island for a reason, and as soon as you figure out what that reason is, then everything—all this pain and suffering you've gone through lately—well, I think it's all going to make a little more sense."

20

Dear Charley,

How best to fill you in on the happenings here in sunny San Juandigo? The first thing to say is that everything is extremely luxurious. I swear I'm pampered every minute, even while I sleep. There are massages, mineral baths, those ridiculous full body seaweed wraps that leave one feeling like a giant sushi roll. Tobit Portnoy—you remember my new friend, the magician, whom I mentioned in my previous emails—well, the other day, Tobit even convinced me to dip my feet into a bucket of baby carp and let them nibble away all the dead skin between my toes. It was a strange sensation to say the least, not unpleasant really, but strange, and afterwards, it felt as if I'd been wearing invisible shoes all my life and had finally just now decided to remove them.

Gastronomically, I want for nothing. Just listen to what I've eaten so far today. For breakfast: room service (complimentary), arriving at my door at the civilized hour of ten. The tray was an artist's palate full of color. Black: a cup of strong hazelnut coffee. Red: two slices of honey toast smeared with Persephone jam. Yellow and white: scrambled eggs covered in thick, creamy gravy.

Lunch, if you can believe it, was even more heavenly. I took it outside on the beach overlooking the sea. Tobit joined me halfway through, and ravished as he was from his morning's snorkel, he devoured all my cucumber sandwiches before I even had a chance to say, "Hello." No matter. The crab salad soon arrived. It was tangy and sweet: tender bits of flesh dressed in a lamb's milk yogurt with lemon juice and candied walnuts thrown in for crunch. We spread the stuff over triangles of warm pita, and for the duration of about fifteen minutes, I wholly believed in the existence of a benevolent God.

I'm sorry if all this has made you hungry. I do hate it whenever I read something about food while I'm not in a position to immediately satiate myself. What is it about us humans that makes us all so prone to desire that which has only just recently been called before our consciousness? And I'm not just talking about stuffing our faces. I mean everything, every stimuli that enters our perception. It's like it's all been specifically designed to trigger something deep inside our reptile brains to make us…to make us…well, to make us *want* for lack of a better word.

This is the trick of Paradise Cruise Lines. It's only taken me a few months to figure it out. What they do is this: first, they say something to you. It can be anything really. A crisp, flavorful lager, for example, or the excitement one experiences at the roulette wheel. When you hear about it, you think, wait a minute, that thing exists and I don't have it. I want it. Then, they give it to you. It's an ingenious scheme. A billion dollar industry has been built around this simple formula, and the devilish thing is, they call their product happiness when in fact it isn't really happiness at all, but actually the absence of happiness, for afterwards, one feels exactly the same as one did before, no better, no worse.

Did you know that they've done studies on the psychology of lottery winners? Tobit was telling me all about it the other day. Apparently, people who become ungodly wealthy overnight—and we're talking hundreds of millions of dollars here, that's *after* taxes—apparently these people report an immediate uptick in happiness, but only for a few months. After that, it's back to life as normal.

I swear, we human beings are strange creatures. Maybe I was wrong before when I said it was our reptile brains that makes us want, for it seems more likely that our desires come to us via the cerebral cortex or else some other part only recently evolved. Is this why animals have no religion, do you think? Have they not yet learned to *want* a God that loves and cares for them and bestows order upon the universe and grants them admission to eternal paradise upon their death?

I'm sorry. This email is rambling and incoherent, but what do you expect from me, since I still haven't received a single word in reply? Not that I'm angry with you, Charley. In fact, I long for you constantly. But unfortunately, you are one of the few desires Paradise Cruise Lines is unable to satisfy, and so here I wait, warm, fat, incredibly comfortable and bored out of my mind, an Odysseus marooned on Calypso's isle. One of these days, I will build a raft and return to you. I shall slaughter all the suitors. Would you like that?

Affectionately yours,
Leo

21

As per his contract with Paradise Cruise Lines, Tobit Portnoy was entitled to a free room at the Atlantis Resort Hotel for the duration of the *Felicity's* stay. Since he was fired because of incompetence and not criminal malfeasance, the benefit remained valid even after his termination. He was no longer garnering a salary, but he was permitted to enjoy all the amenities regularly offered to the resort's guests, which was a pretty sweet deal, considering he'd nearly incinerated a woman and sent another to the sick bay.

Now that all his shows were cancelled, Tobit had a great deal of time on his hands. We took many of our meals together and often held long conversations regarding all manner of topics. He proved himself to be a very intelligent young man. Though raised Baptist, he was extremely interested in the Catholic Church, specifically in the breadth and exactness of our catechism. He also loved the history of ecumenical councils. He knew every major heresy by heart and all the arguments for and against them. His favorite was Docetism, the idea that Jesus's physical body was not actually real but merely an illusion, like an elaborate magic trick pulled off by the Holy Spirit. This belief, he said, was unequivocally rejected at the First Council of Nicaea in 325 AD, but that didn't stop him from wondering about it even today.

"Like what even constitutes a *real* body, you know? Flesh? Blood? The ability to grow? The capacity to suffer? According to the Gospel of John, Thomas refused to believe in the risen Christ until he'd personally stuck his finger into Jesus's wounds. When Jesus showed up, Thomas changed his tune, of course, but then John didn't actually say that Thomas *touched* Jesus, only that he *saw* him and believed. And anyway, what kind of physical body can just up and pass through locked doors? You know what I mean, Fr. Murphy? What are we to make of *that*?"

I told Tobit was wasting his time with all this nonsense. Docetism. Arianism. Sabellianism. Psilianthropism. What was the point of arguing over stupid details when belief itself was so ridiculous?

Tobit responded, not without some pleasure, I think, that I myself was a heretic now, and so I should be more open to alternative theologies.

"Listen, I wrote about killing Christ. I didn't split hairs over the nature of his divinity."

"Yes, but that's the wrong way to look at it. The devil is in the details, Fr. Murphy. So is God."

It was these sorts of tête-à-têtes—equal parts intellectual and inane—that led me to seek out Tobit's company whenever I wearied of resort life. One morning about five weeks into our stay, I decided to pay him a visit. I had just sent Charley what was now my *thirty-sixth* unanswered email, and I don't know if it was her silence or my restlessness or perhaps even divine inspiration, but I had recently made up my mind to do something sort of crazy, and I wanted his help pulling it off.

"Hello? Hello, Tobit, are you in there?" No answer from inside his suite. The door was ajar, so I pushed it open. "There you are. Turn around and listen, will you? I've come to tell you something that...wait a minute, what the hell's going on in here?"

108

"Oh, hello, Fr. Murphy. Sit down. You can help if you'd like."

It wasn't immediately clear what kind of "help" Tobit had in mind. He was kneeling on the floor in front of the TV with a collection of US highway maps spread out all around him. These maps covered nearly every available inch of his suite. Tobit's bed had been pushed against the far wall to make room for Texas, his dresser relocated to the closet so as not to disturb California. Tobit himself was currently most interested in the Southwest portion of the country. Examining the deserts of Arizona and New Mexico, he dangled a chain above these states at the end of which was suspended a crystal the size of a walnut.

I asked him again what the hell he was doing.

"Dowsing," he said. "You know, divination." He showed me the chain with the crystal attached. "This is my pendulum. Pretty cool, huh? Now sit down. It works better with someone else asking the question."

Before I knew what I'd gotten myself into, I was on the floor just west of San Antonio getting a full lecture on the magic of remote location. Dowsing was a practice with a long and intricate history, I was told. Its equipment (rods, pendulums, bones, etc.) was as varied as the treasures one could search for. For hundreds of years, prospectors and pirates, explorers and aspiring tycoons had all tapped into this mystical power, hoping to discover riches beyond their wildest dreams, and now Tobit was trying his hand to find a girl.

"So the way this works is simple, Fr. Murphy. I'm going to sit here, deep in meditation, holding this pendulum over the map. Whenever you're ready, I need you to ask, 'Where's Madonna Garfield?' and then the crystal will show us where she is."

"You mean it'll move?"

"Uh-huh."

"Completely on its own? No funny business?"

"This isn't a trick. I'm worried about my girlfriend. I want to make sure she's alright."

I asked wouldn't it be easier to call or send an email, and he said that he'd tried both many times but with no response.

"So now you've resorted to supernatural stalking?"

"It isn't stalking. It's locating."

"I don't know. Seems like a fine distinction."

"Look," said Tobit, "I get that Madonna might be busy or needs space or whatever, but it's been a long time since I've heard from her, and it would, you know, put my mind at ease, if I at least knew she was still in Tucson."

"As opposed to where? Floating dead in the middle of the Pacific Ocean?"

He gave me a nasty look.

"Alight, fine. I'll play along. You don't have to get all bent out of shape over there. Now what am I supposed to say again? Just, "Madonna Garfield?' Not 'Madonna Garfield, previously of Mount Sinai?' or, 'Madonna Garfield, the dreaded cow murderer?' I don't know how specific the dark spirits need me to be."

Tobit said "Madonna Garfield" would work just fine. Then he closed his eyes and extended his arm over the highway maps and began humming in a full, low-pitched tone, which normally would've sent me into hysterics or at least elicited some wry comment. The reason I kept silent: it occurred to me that Tobit and I weren't so different in our respective situations. Here we were, both homeless, broke, recently fired, and in love with women who, given all available evidence, probably didn't love us back. The only thing that distinguished us was age. I had more of it, and was thus cranky and intolerable. Tobit had less of it, and was therefore a moron.

"Okay, let's get this over with. Dear spirits of the netherworld, Leopold Murphy here, fellow heretic and blasphemer. If you aren't too busy poking holes in condoms or whatever it is you do to pass the time, would you mind directing this pendulum thingy in the direction of Madonna Garfield? She's the girl with the black nail polish and charming personality, if you haven't already met. My friend would like to know where she's currently residing, so…that's all I've got."

I waited in silence while Tobit suspended the crystal over the maps. Though nothing happened for a very long time, he didn't stop humming or open his eyes. I kept my mouth shut for my part. Then, after maybe three or four minutes, the pendulum started moving in small, clockwise circles. At first, the rotations were so subtle I might've missed them had I not been staring, but then they grew larger and larger until soon the crystal was describing a wide aerial route over the deserts of southern Arizona. Obviously Tobit was moving the pendulum himself, and even if I couldn't actually discern the slight trembling of his hand, I wasn't about to believe any of this hocus pocus bullshit. Nevertheless, I will admit to a certain theatrical satisfaction when over the course of the next ninety seconds or so, the circles reversed course, growing tighter and tighter until finally coming to rest directly above the city of Tucson.

"Well, there you have it," I said. "You invoked the dark spirits, and they told you what you wanted to hear. You can stop worrying now. Madonna's still in college, and I feel like a real idiot for my 'dead in Pacific Ocean' hypothesis."

Tobit just frowned. He dropped the pendulum onto the map and then leaned back against the wall.

"What's the matter?" I asked him. "I thought Tucson was good news?"

"You really don't get it, do you?"

I said I guess I didn't. All this magic nonsense was his territory.

He looked at me, and when he spoke next, his voice was clipped and full of emotion like he might break down crying at any moment. "Why hasn't she written, Fr. Murphy? She promised she would. Every day, she said. But it's been so long and I've heard nothing. I want you to be honest with me. Do you think it's stupid what I'm doing? I mean, do I really have any good reason to believe she still cares about me?"

Let it be noted that under normal circumstances, I might've told the boy the cold hard truth of the matter and then left him wallowing there with his broken heart. But just as I had previously restrained myself from laughing at his divination routine, so, too, did I keep my cruel words unspoken. Instead, I crawled over the carpet and sat next to him against the wall. Patting his shoulder in a comforting, paternal kind of way, I said, "Hey, stop that now, alright? Keep your goddamn chin up. This is Madonna Garfield we're talking about, not some ten cent whore."

Tobit sucked a nosefull of mucus back into his throat.

"Listen, you're the most faithful, optimistic, blissfully romantic person I've ever met outside of maybe Jerry Campbell, may he rest in peace. Now if you start having doubts, then where does that leave the rest of us? Specifically, where does that leave me?"

"What are you talking about?"

I told him I meant Charley, of course, and my delusional fantasy that one day we might still end up together.

"But Charley loves you, Fr. Murphy. I know she does."

"There you go. There's that unfounded optimism we've all come to know and love."

Tobit said it wasn't unfunded. It was just his opinion. Meanwhile, he and Madonna—

"Meanwhile, you and Madonna have a much better shot of making it. I'm serious. Just consider the cases objectively. On the one hand, we have a girl who loves you so much she was willing to slaughter your father's cow and then feed it to him. On the other hand, we have a woman who wouldn't even run away with me when I asked her to come to New York. And New York was her dream. She always wanted to write for

Broadway. It's not like I asked her to go to Detroit or something. So anyway, the bottom line is this. If you're going to continue this stubbornness regarding me and Charley, then you're going to have to keep faith in you and Madonna, too. It's only fair. Otherwise, I'll think you're just lying to me to spare my feelings, which isn't actually nice in the long run. You understand?"

Tobit dabbed some tears from his eyes. He nodded and said he understood. "Thank you, Fr. Murphy."

"Right, well, you're welcome, I guess, but keep in mind I'm just giving you the facts of the matter. No reason to get all gooey. Anyway, I came here to ask for a favor."

"Oh?" said Tobit. "Well, sure. Whatever I can do."

I glanced around his suite, making a quick survey. "You don't happen to have a map of San Juandigo, do you?"

He said he did actually. He got up and retrieved it from his dresser. "Are you trying to find something?"

"Not something," I told him. "*Someone.*"

22

The thing you had to understand about my brother was that he'd always been a touch unstable. My theory was that it went back to childhood when our mother died via postpartum hemorrhage just minutes after Stephen was born. Since her passing broke our father (emotionally, spiritually, financially, etc.), it was basically up to me to raise my little brother, which maybe explains why he turned out so fucked up. Of all us Murphy's, Stephen was the only atheist, or at least the only one who was a prick about it. He founded the Rational Thinkers Club his junior year at St. Ignatius (this was my first year in seminary), which scandalized a lot of the older Jesuits, though from what I heard, it was just him and a couple of his loser friends sitting around an empty classroom, quoting Nietzsche to each other.

Okay, so maybe he was no great philosopher, but Stephen was otherwise a genius when it came to school. He earned a scholarship, then a bachelors, and eventually a doctorate from the University of Chicago where he studied evolutionary biology and genetics. This was where he met Gertrude, his first wife, a pale, thin, strikingly beautiful woman who spoke very politely to your face and then said cutting, judgmental things behind your back. Gertrude was also an atheist and a biologist. She studied plants, which I guess made sense as they were the only organisms she could relate to. When they weren't working on their research, she and Stephen would do pretentious cultural things around the city like attending experimental jazz concerts or trying out all the hot new vegan restaurants. I never understood why, but my brother was infatuated with this woman. He spoke of her constantly whenever I called and made it clear (in a patronizing tone of voice only a "rational thinker" could pull off) that while he and Gertrude disagreed with me vis-à-vis the whole God issue, they still respected my opinion in a purely anthropological sense.

Thank God Stephen left this woman shortly after I moved from St. Raphael's to St. Peter's. This was the one good thing about that otherwise shitty year. The reason for the change (Stephen's, not mine) was a sudden and dramatic conversion to the Christian faith. My brother had "found" Jesus as they say, and then promptly "lost" Gertrude. His new wife Kitty (real name Katherine) was a portly, good-natured (if simple-minded) blonde, whom you might know better as "The Biblical Baketress" if you've ever ordered religiously-themed birthday cakes from her over the internet. After marrying Kitty, Stephen resigned from his tenure-track faculty position and began his second career from which he became considerably richer and more famous. Perhaps you've seen his DVDs or heard him lecture at one of the many evangelical colleges that pepper the southern region of this fine country? A one-time disciple of Charles Darwin, Stephen rededicated his career to Creationism, using his background as an evolutionary biologist to argue for a literal interpretation of Genesis.

The last time I saw him wasn't actually in person, but on the TV screen in the rectory of St. Peter's. Charley had discovered one of his DVDs under my bed and wanted to watch the thing, which we did despite my protests. This particular lecture (*Charles Darwin and the Religion of Death Part IV*) was filmed at some mega-church in Texas, the kind of place where communion wafers are bought in bulk and strange octopus-looking tube machines fill about five thousand shot glasses with grape juice every Sunday.

Stephen was a showman if nothing else. He strut around the altar in his fine blue suit, wearing one of those hands-free microphones pop-singers wear, clicking through a series of Powerpoint slides that displayed "evidence" on a huge projection screen suspended from the rafters. Charley got a kick out of the whole performance, but personally, I was too pissed-off to find anything funny about it. Watching the DVD, I was reminded of my first year at St. Peter's (this was around the time my brother was becoming famous) when I used to get regular packages from him in the mail. Kitty would send along one of her cakes (Cain murdering Abel, Jacob stealing Esau's blessing), while Stephen included his latest lecture series, which I would watch alone, sadomasochisticly, sipping a cocktail of vehemence and spite and sometimes also a real cocktail mixed with proportionally more alcohol than was standard.

Alright, I was jealous. I admit it.

It's not that I wanted to *be* Stephen exactly, but I did wish my brother was less successful in general. You have to remember that this was a period of rough transition in my life. I'd just moved from Chicago to Chippewa County to begin my assignment at St. Peter's, which was a very different church from St. Raphael's. Despite the surrounding poverty, I'd been quite happy serving at the latter, for there was purpose in my ministry there. I knew I was doing the work of God, and this was the whole reason I'd become a priest to begin with.

But such was not the case at St. Peter's. In Chippewa County, I felt more like a glorified business manager than a man of the cloth. Case in point, I spent a lot of time in finance meetings. I was responsible for the budget, which was a big job considering there was actually money to manage at this church. Often I butted heads with parishioners who wanted things like new pews with more comfortable kneelers. On Sundays, my impassioned, quasi-Marxist homilies usually fell flat. Given the circumstances, was it any wonder that I fell into depression? My friendship with Jerry Campbell, my love for his wife, these weren't enough to save me. Gradually, I grew bitter as the world became a darker and darker place.

But enough of this gloomy business. Like I said before, the primary reason I'd come to San Juandigo was to learn how to be happy again, and it had dawned on me slowly over the course of many weeks that empty comforts such as those offered at the Atlantis Resort Hotel and Casino were never going to satisfy me in this regard. No, if I was going to return to Charley a changed man, I'd need to take a more proactive role in my well-being, and what better way to accomplish this than by reconciling with my long lost brother?

I believe I mentioned earlier that Stephen had come to the island many months ago in order to finance and oversee the reconstruction of the children's hospital. My brother's vast wealth allowed him to do things like this. He was a regular philanthropist these days, jetting all over the world, fighting malaria, dolling out peanut butter to hungry children, etc. It wasn't lost on me, this amazing coincidence, that after so many years estranged, Stephen and I had managed to wind up on the same patch of rock in the middle of the ocean. But was it a coincidence really, or was there something else at work here, some divine providence guiding us back together?

Or is that sort of talk just a little bit crazy?

23

"Crazy," said Dr. Talia Mayrose. "Certifiably insane. Don't even talk to me about Stephen Murphy. The last I saw him, it was months ago, and then poof, gone, he disappears without warning or explanation, and there's still half a hospital left to build, not that we can do a damn thing about it without his money. Do you know how difficult it is to treat patients when everyone's jammed under these tents and I have to pick through the rubble just to get some decent supplies?"

With a breath of exasperation, she brushed past us carrying her clipboard, gauze, antibiotics and whatever else she'd managed to scrounge that morning. Talia didn't walk so much as fly through the camp, while the children—there were hundreds of them—were so preoccupied with their own suffering that they hardly even noticed her speeding by.

"Isabel? Isabel, look at me."

Talia paused over one of the cots where there lay a small, dark-skinned girl around six years of age. The child was missing the bottom half of her left leg, and the bandage wrapped around the nub was discolored and smelled foul.

"Isabel, I need a response from you."

The little girl failed to stir.

"Isabel, sit up or I'm leaving," said Talia. "I don't have time for this. You either want to live or you don't. Decide right

118

now, because I'm not giving you any more painkillers if you're just going to lie there and die."

Tobit looked at me, clearly shaken. This was not the kind of doctor we'd expected to find here. Just a few hours earlier, the Atlantis Resort concierge (a delightful woman named Judith) had informed us that while San Juandigo's new hospital was under construction, the temporary field unit was being staffed by a crack team of volunteer physicians, some real Florence Nightingale types. Talia, however, was ragged, prickly, and obviously sleep-deprived. Instead of wearing the traditional white coat of her profession, she had on dusty blue jeans and a grey t-shirt. Her face was tanned a deep bronze color, and so were her forearms and the semi-circle of skin just under her neck. What little of her hair that was visible snaking from her canvas bush hat was knotty and unclean. Her whole body smelled kind of not great. She had the stink of medicine about her.

"Isn't there anything you can do?" said Tobit. His eyes had turned soft over the little girl in the cot. "She seems to be in real pain. Maybe if you gave her some—"

"Look, kid, let me tell you how this is going to work." Talia cast an annoyed glance over her clipboard. "You're going to stand there quietly and keep your opinions to yourself. Meanwhile, the medical professional is going to make a medical decision. Would I like to give the child painkillers? Of course I would. I would also like a magic wand I could wave to make the infection in her leg go away. But I don't have a magic wand, and I barely have any painkillers, so unless Isabel starts showing some sign of life—you hear me, Isabel? Unless you start showing some sign of life—I'm going to continue walking down this row until I find someone who hasn't given up yet."

Tobit stared blankly at the doctor. Then he turned to me and whispered, "Do something, Fr. Murphy."

"Like what?"

"I don't know. Pray. Give a blessing. *Something.*"

The best I could manage was a lame shrug.

Tobit sighed and shook his head. Taking matters into his own hands, he reached into his pocket and produced a shiny new quarter, which he held up so that Isabel could see. "Behold, an ordinary coin. I want you to look very closely now because something amazing's about to happen."

The little girl remained motionless while he tapped the quarter many times against the backside of his left hand, "trying to find the soft spot," he explained. Then Tobit said, "Ah, there it is," and with a quick flash of showmanship, he pushed the coin through his flesh until it popped out the other side, toppling from his open palm and onto the cot beside the child. It was a neat trick, really, but Isabel didn't react at all.

"Right," said Talia. "Well, now that that's over with—"

"Hold on," said Tobit, undismayed. He had performed for far tougher audiences and was not about to give up so easily. He picked up the quarter again and began rolling it along the top of his knuckles, an impressive feat in its own right. After a few passes, he placed the coin directly upon Isabel's stomach and said, "Nice belly button."

The child's eyelids fluttered.

"There you go. Now you're getting into the show. But don't tell me you're one of those navel-gazers who's only interested in her own affairs. Don't misunderstand, there's nothing wrong with a little self-reflection, but take it from me, if you spend your whole life concerned with *numero uno*, then you're going to miss out on one big fantastic world out there."

Talia scrawled a few notes down on her clipboard, exhaling impatiently.

Isabel still hadn't moved enough to earn her medicine.

Tobit began passing his hands back and forth over her belly, his palms hovering just inches above the quarter. He said, "Let me take care of that for you. You know, presumably one can't navel-gaze without a navel."

It happened faster than the eye could register. One moment, the coin was there. The next, it had vanished.

"There's nothing magic about making money disappear," said Talia, but despite her cynicism, the trick had elicited from Isabel the child's first discernable expression, a kind of half smile half frown, more parts confusion than delight.

Tobit winked at her and said, "Where did it go?"

No answer from the girl.

"Is it behind your ear, do you think? In my experience, folks are always leaving coins behind their ears. A sign of poor hygiene, if you ask me. Do you mind if I..." He leaned over the child now, his massive torso not unlike the trunk of some great redwood suspended mid timber. "No, don't trouble yourself. I think I see it. Oh dear. Oh dear. Well, this couldn't possibly be right."

"What is it?" I said, surprised to be playing along.

Tobit glanced at me, equally surprised, but no less grateful for the assistance. "It's really something, Fr. Murphy. I've never seen a case like this before. We might need to consult an ear, nose, and throat specialist. Dr. Mayrose, you wouldn't happen to know..."

"Just get on with it," said Talia.

Tobit turned back to Isabel, emboldened now that the little girl's eyes had grown wide with incredulity. He put his hand behind her ear and made a show off pulling out the quarter.

"It won't budge," he said, huffing with exertion. "It's down deep, you see? It's stuck. There's just too many...oh, hold on. Wait a minute now. I think I might just—oops!"

This time I really couldn't tell how he pulled it off. The quarter-through-palm and quarter-off-belly maneuvers, those were some nifty tricks, but this here was magic of a different kind. No sooner had Tobit thrown himself backwards in a sort of Farley-esque pratfall than about two hundred silver coins began spilling from Isabel's ears and into her cot. The child leapt up at once, either out of fear or wonderment, it was hard

121

to say. She put both hands to her ears, not that it mattered, for the quarters just kept coming, slipping through her fingers and down her arms, while Tobit—really milking the scene for all it was worth—climbed back to his feet and began rubbing his rear end pathetically. He looked down at Isabel like a plumber considering a blown faucet. The expression on his face was like, "Well, shit, this situation is beyond me." Then a truly wonderful thing happened. The little girl smiled. She took her hands from her ears and ran them through the piles of quarters on either side of her. Gradually, the coins stopped falling from wherever it was they were falling, and in the quiet that followed, all we could hear was Isabel's soft laughter.

"Wonderful," said Talia, breaking the spell. She set her sack down on the cot next to Isabel's bandaged leg and began removing fresh gauze and antibiotics and painkillers. "You know, if you were going to make money appear, you didn't have to stop with quarters. You'll be leaving those here, by the way. Consider it payment for putting me behind schedule."

Tobit said he had no problem with such an arrangement. He was grinning from ear to ear, as was Isabel. In fact, now that she'd witnessed what may as well have been a real miracle, the little girl looked brighter and more alive than ever. While Talia cleaned her wound and changed her bandages, we lingered just off to the side, peppering the doctor with further questions regarding my brother. Talia, however, had no more information to pass along. As far as Stephen's motives or mental health or current whereabouts were concerned, our guess was as good as hers.

She left us soon after. With no idea what to do next, Tobit and I wandered out of the camp and over to the half-constructed hospital which stood about a hundred yards to the east. I won't pretend it wasn't a relief to get away from all those sick and dying children, but lingering there amongst the skeletons of construction, I began to feel deeply uneasy.

"Thinking about all that money you stole?" said Tobit.

"Huh?"

"The cash Jerry won for eating those hamburgers. Wasn't it supposed to go to rebuilding this place? And instead you used it to take a vacation. I was just wondering if you were feeling guilty now we're out here and you've seen the consequences first hand. I only ask because it looks like something's troubling you."

"Oh," I said. "Well actually I was thinking about Stephen, but now that you mention it, I guess that was a pretty rotten thing for me to do."

Tobit said he was sorry for bringing it up.

"It's alright," I told him. After all, I deserved far worse than a prickly reminder every once in a while.

"Strange news about your brother, though."

"Yeah."

"Any idea what might've happened?"

I shrugged.

"Hm," said Tobit. "Well, we can't just give up now. There's got to be someone here who knows where he went. Did Stephen have any friends on this island? Any colleagues?"

I reminded him that I hadn't spoken to my brother in years. I didn't even have his phone number, for Christ's sakes.

"Right. Well, that does make things more difficult."

Tobit sat down on a pile of steel beams and thought silently for a long while. I was just about to tell him that it was hopeless and that we might as well call a cab to take us back to the hotel when a loud *bang* rang out though the air. It wasn't a gunshot or anything like that, just some car backfiring. An old jeep actually. I spotted it on the road leading away from the camp where it was sputtering to its death at approximately two miles an hour.

"How about that," said Tobit, rising to his feet with a wistful smile. "Look who it is, Fr. Murphy. Our old friend, Bembé."

Sure enough, as soon as the jeep was dead, Bembé Villanueva—the soon-to-be missionary we'd met weeks ago in the market—leapt from the driver seat and popped the hood. When a belch of black smoke rose ominously from the innards, Bembé took two steps back. The poor kid was clearly bewildered.

"Let's go help him," said Tobit.

"Sure," I said, following quickly behind. Though I harbored no illusions regarding my prowess in the automotive realm, I could at least offer some moral support and maybe even an apology for being kind of a dick the last time we spoke.

Bembé greeted us with a warm smile as we drew near. "Fr. Murphy, Brother Tobit, good afternoon to you both. What a pleasant surprise to see you in this part of the island! Most tourists, I'm sorry to say, keep mainly to the resort, which is a shame, for San Juandigo is large and full of wonders. I can tell that you two are much more adventurous in your travels. No wonder, being men of faith. It is written: 'If I take the wings of the morning and dwell in the uttermost parts of the sea, even there your hand shall lead me.' You don't happen to know anything about automotive repair, do you?"

Bembé's hopefulness was immediately rewarded, for Tobit said yes, actually he did have some experience in this matter, given that he'd grown up on a ranch where tractors and trucks and all sorts of other machinery were always breaking down.

"Alleluia! The young lions suffer want and hunger, but those who seek the Lord lack no good thing."

"This kid's got a verse for literally any situation."

"What's that?" said Bembé.

"Nothing," I told him. "Go ahead, Tobit. Make yourself useful if you've got the know-how."

While he leaned over Bembé's jeep, I asked our friend what he was doing in these parts, and he said he came for the sick children. Every day, after selling fruit in the market,

Bembé would drive eight miles to the camp and then spend a few hours praying with the little boys and girls who would soon be dead. He'd been doing this ever since the earthquake, and he planned to keep doing it until the day he left for Seminary.

"Must be kind of depressing," I said, "to be surrounded by so much pain and suffering."

Bembé said no, just because the children were sick, that didn't make them miserable.

Tobit popped his head up from the engine. His brow was dripping sweat, and his cheeks were black from all the smoke, but a wide smile stretched across his face.

"Should be no problem at all. You got a toolbox, Bembé? All I need is a wrench."

While the kid fetched the necessary instruments, he asked me the same question I'd asked him: what were we doing out here, so far from the resort?

"Ah, well, that's a long story, actually. The short version is that we were looking for my brother, but of course he's making things difficult by having gone completely AWOL."

"Oh? Who's your brother?"

"Funny thing: you might've met him. Stephen Murphy? He's white, of course, about my height, richer than God, possesses a generally douchey personality."

Bembé's face changed at the exact moment Tobit got the jeep to turn over. One second, he was perfectly content, the next, it was like I'd spoken the name of Satan, or at least one of his lesser compatriots. Hot, sooty gasses spewed hellishly from the jeep's exhaust while the kid backed away slowly, his hands trembling with what I could only assume to be fear.

"So you do know him?"

"Oh, yes, I'm afraid I do."

"And do you know where he is now?"

He hesitated a moment before nodding yes.

"Well, what do you know?" I said to Tobit. "The kid's proved himself useful after all."

24

You'll want to consider this for context:

About fifteen minutes into *Charles Darwin and the Religion of Death, Part IV*, Dr. Stephen Murphy stands at the pulpit wearing a navy blue suit and red tie. He holds a laser-pointer. There is a bottle of water in front of him alongside his notes. Behind him, a large white screen has been pulled down over the wall, and projected onto this screen is the first of his fifty or so PowerPoint slides. The current slide reads, "And God saw that it was good," which is a quote from Genesis. The words are in big blue block letters pasted over a painting of the Garden of Eden. Stephen clears his throat and gives a warm smile to those assembled. The camera pans across the audience. A lot of overweight people here. A woman (Sunday dress pulled over her girth like a tropical parachute) fans herself with an open hymnal. Her husband has one of those guts that just keeps on going. Everybody's sweating and excited and well-dressed and packed in tight. The camera cuts back to Stephen who is no longer behind the pulpit but instead walking easily back and forth across the altar under the big projection screen. He waves and smiles. He points to people in the audience. He's got his laser-pointer in one hand and his bottle of water (now opened) in the other. He says, "Thank you, thank you, God bless, thank you, God bless, thank you all." Everyone is cheering for him. The camera pulls back as far as it can to show as much of the church as it can. "Thank you, thank you all, God bless, God bless, God bless."

Cut back to Stephen. He's stopped pacing. He takes a big drink of water. Stephen drinks water constantly, like all day, like three or four times the amount recommended by doctors. Ever since he was little, he's done this, which maybe accounts for the bed-wetting well past his eleventh birthday. I have to admit: he's in incredibly good shape for a man his age (43 at the time this particular DVD was recorded). He doesn't look a day over thirty. He holds up both hands like he's pushing away the crowd and pulling them forward in the same motion. He gives a wide smile to show that's he the happiest, most blessed man in the whole world. Finally, the crowd grows quiet. Fifteen thousand faithful asses squeeze back into the pews. Stephen looks out over his flock. The first thing he says is, "I've got a riddle for you all. A real head-scratcher." He pauses for dramatic effect. Stephen is nothing if not a showman. The camera cuts to various close ups of the assembled: a man wearing a seersucker suit and a pastel bowtie who is obviously gay but refusing to accept it, a young blonde woman with the wide-eyed stupidity of a high school cheerleader, a cancer patient with bald head, oxygen mask, oxygen tank. The camera cuts back to Stephen. He takes a big drink from his water bottle and smacks his lips and says, "Ahhh." Then he says, "Who here can tell me the difference between a terrorist and an evolutionary biologist?" This gets a chuckle from the crowd. Stephen clicks his laser-pointer, which has a button on the end so that it also controls the PowerPoint. The slide switches to reveal two side by side photographs, one of Osama Bin Laden, one of Richard Dawkins. There is some booing and hissing.

Stephen says, "You can negotiate with a terrorist."

This gets a big laugh from the congregation. Stephen points the laser-pointer at the screen. A red dot appears on the forehead of Osama Bin Laden. He makes a gunshot sound.

Some cheers. Then he moves the red dot over the forehead of Richard Dawkins and makes another gunshot sound. Bigger cheers this time. "If only it were that easy," says Stephen, and clicks the button on his laser-pointer to change slides. Now the picture on the screen is one of Earth as seen from space.

"Isn't she beautiful?"

He's moving again, walking back and forth across the altar with the easy gait of a senator charming his way through a filibuster. He repeats himself: "Isn't she beautiful?" and gets some "yes sirs" and "uh-huhs" this time. He clicks his laser-pointer to change slides. A cartoon Earth (which is also a woman, you can tell, because of the locks of blonde hair curling down the Americas and Eastern Europe) is blowing out the candles of a birthday cake. Stephen says, "Now I'm sure the gentlemen here can back me up on this. It's always—and I mean *always*—rude to ask a woman her age."

More laughter from the flock, which turns gradually into applause. Stephen takes a drink from his water bottle. He smacks his lips, says "Ah." Then he says, "But you know what's even ruder than that? What's even ruder is to take a pretty little planet like this, just six thousand years young, and go around pretending she's an old maid!"

Another click of the old laser-pointer. The cartoon Earth isn't looking so good in this one. She's slumped over in a wheel chair, wearing reading glasses, and knitting a sweater. Overhead the words read, "Scientists estimate Earth's age at 4.6 billion years."

"Really?" says Stephen. "4.6 billion years?"

He whistles that way people whistle when they hear a really big number, usually with a dollar sign attached. The whistling is contagious. Pretty soon everybody in the church is whistling.

Stephen says, "Here's a word of advice. If anybody ever tells you they know what was going on 4.6 billion years ago, take it with a grain of salt." He clicks the laser-pointer. The next slide shows Richard Dawkins lecturing at some university in the UK. There's a giant saltshaker hovering over his head which tilts over and pours just a ton of salt on top of him. It gathers in a pile around his legs. It climbs to his chest. It doesn't stop until poor Richard's buried up to his neck. A little speech bubble pops out of his mouth that says, "HELP!"

"And by that I mean a mountain of salt."

The folks at the mega church are really eating this shit up. The energy is electric. I have to admit (though by this point I feel like throwing a brick through my TV) that Stephen knows how to work his audience. He blitzes through a series of slides, lambasting the "Voodoo practice" of carbon-dating. He refers to the fossil record as the "Gospel of Death."

Some ninety minutes later: "This is the most important thing I've come here today to tell you."

Stephen pauses under the projection screen, taking one last dramatic gulp of water before casting the bottle aside along with the six others which litter the altar. A reverent and expectant hush falls over the church. My brother has come to his last slide of the presentation, a cartoonist's rendering of Adam and Eve (complete with modesty leaves) standing before the Tree of Knowledge. If you look hard, you can see the serpent slithering around the trunk.

"Some of you might be wondering to yourself, what's the difference. Am I right? You're thinking, 'Okay, you've convinced me, Dr. Murphy. Darwinism, no matter what it pretends to be, is a religion like any other. But so then what? Why should I put my faith in Jesus, who demands hard things from me, when I can just as easily trust in science and live a life of comfort and pleasure?'"

Stephen pauses again to let the words sink in. I don't know what the hell he means by science leading to "a life of comfort and pleasure" (especially considering his mind-breaking tenure push just a few years earlier), but as the camera pans over the audience, all you see is quiet, thoughtful nodding.

"The difference," says Stephen, "between Christianity and Darwinism is the difference between life and death, and I mean that literally." He begins pacing again, slowly at first, but gaining speed. "Think about it. We Christian believe in Genesis. We believe in God. We believe that by His very outpouring of love, He spoke the universe into being as a good and harmonious thing. We believe he created Man and Woman in his own image. We believe he set us in dominion over the whole world. But we also believe that we failed in our duty. We believe that we sinned against God, and that this sin brought death and destruction into a universe, and that we need Jesus Christ to redeem us."

He pauses again under the projection screen, looking up at the cartoonist's rendering of Adam and Eve. He shakes his head as if to say, "You let us down you two, but then again, could I have done any better?" The whole church has grown silent.

"This is not what science teaches," says Stephen. "Whereas Christianity values the goodness and dignity of all life, Darwin proclaims that only through death—years and years and years of death and evolution—can a species ever hope to reach a state of perfection. This is why the Earth must be 4.6 billion years old. Because it takes time, an incredible, unbelievable amount of time, for so much death to build up. This," says Stephen, clicking the button on the end of his laser-pointer, "this is Darwin's Garden of Eden."

It's another animation. Adam and Eve, up there on the projection screen, feel the earth shaking under their feet. They look at each other, worried. Suddenly, the ground gives way as the Garden of Eden vomits up piles and piles of dead animals. There are monkeys, lions, bears, elephants, zebras, wolves, dinosaurs of all variety, saber-tooth tigers with x's over their eyes, decapitated mastodons. It's like Noah's Ark capsized into a tar pit and then exploded. It's chaos, carnage. The crowd is loving it. Stephen has to shout over the cheers to be heard.

"What kind of garden is this?"

He's pacing back and forth across the altar like crazy. Empty plastic water bottles crackle under his feet. His notes fly through the air.

"What kind of garden is this?"

You would think the question is purely rhetorical, but the way he says it, the way he *insists* upon it, it's as if Stephen is demanding an answer, but from whom it's unclear.

"What kind of garden is this?"

It's no garden, is what it is. Not anymore. It's a mountain of corpses, and it keeps growing. It's a whole zoo. You can't even see Adam and Eve. They're somewhere in the stratosphere now, pushed up past the upper limits of the screen.

"What kind of garden is this?" says Stephen.

His voice is hoarse from screaming. He's on his knees now, a man stripped bare.

"What kind of garden?"

25

La Mantaña Embrujada was a wicked place. Sheer, treacherous, uninhabited for centuries, the mountain towered over the western half of San Juandigo, casting a long, dark shadow on the people below. Most islanders refused to come within a quarter mile of the peak—they claimed it was the last refuge of the old gods—and if they did happen to be passing by, they would shut their mouths and hold their noses so as not to breathe in the poisoned air. Bembé, who was no superstitious fool, agreed to drive us the ten miles from the hospital camp to the base of the mountain, but even he refused to accompany us further.

"And why not?" I asked him. "Don't tell me you believe in these ghost stories?"

He remained silent while gravel crunched under the tires of his jeep. It was dark now, and because his headlights were dim, we had to drive slowly or else risk winding up in the ditch.

"What does that even mean?" said Tobit from the backseat. "Refuge of the old gods?"

Bembé spoke very quietly: "Before Juandigo, this island was subject to all manner of spirits. There were dozens of temples and many priests, but no matter how faithfully the people worshipped, the gods were cruel to them, sending hurricanes and earthquakes, diseases, famine. Then when the white man from across the sea arrived, he spoke of a God who ruled above all others, yet the people were loath to give up the old gods, for all the priests had warned them that their betrayal would only bring about further pain and suffering. 'Why trust this pale stranger?' they asked. 'What does he know about our land?'"

I noticed that Bembé's fingers had tightened around the steering wheel as he spoke. He eyes were darting back and forth amongst the trees. From the surrounding woods came the buzz of insects and the howling of nocturnal monkeys.

"One day, a large crate washed up on shore from the ship that had delivered Juandigo. The people sent for the Jesuit that he might open it. Inside, he discovered a sword, a shield, and a suit of armor, all miraculously untouched by seawater. 'God has sent me these arms that I might drive out your false gods,' he told them. 'Tonight, I shall visit all the temples of this island and do battle so that tomorrow we might all bend a knee to the one true Lord.'"

"And then what happened?" asked Tobit.

"Juandigo did as he promised," said Bembé. "He battled all through the night, and in the end, he drove the old gods from their temples. But now they have flown here to *La Mantaña Embrujada*. You would do well to tread lightly upon this peak. Even holy men are not safe. Now please get out. I can take you no further."

He put the jeep into park and left the engine running. Try as we might, we could not persuade him to come with us, though he did point us in the direction of a narrow path, which snaked up the mountain and led to my brother's cabin. He also gave us two working flashlights for the journey.

"Thank you," said Tobit as we climbed out. "We'll return these as soon as we can."

"You just worry about returning yourselves. I won't miss the flashlights."

After Bembé had driven off, we started our trek up the mountain. I could tell Tobit was a bit spooked now that we were alone. When a monkey howled in the distance, he jumped and pointed his flashlight at the noise.

"Calm down, won't you? Old gods, cursed mountain, it's all superstitious nonsense."

"That might be true, Fr. Murphy, but I'd feel a lot better if I had Juandigo's sword with me."

"You're the size of a bull elephant. If any spirits attack, just put them in a headlock."

We continued up the path, which was winding and steep and overgrown with roots. In daylight, it would've proved a difficult hike. In the darkness, it was downright treacherous.

"Careful here. Watch those loose rocks."

"Thank you, Fr. Murphy."

"You'll want to keep that flashlight on the ground in front of us, not off in the trees."

"Right."

"You aren't doing it."

"No offense, but when the old gods attack, they won't be coming from the ground in front of us."

We traveled in silence for some time. The higher we climbed, the steeper the grade, and soon we were both out of breath. To be completely honest, it wasn't just the path that worried me. Gods and ghosts I could manage, but there were other creatures in the woods tonight, large ones, and I don't just mean the monkeys that wouldn't shut up.

"Are there any big cats native to the Caribbean?" asked Tobit, as if he'd been reading my mind.

I told him I had no idea.

"I think there might be jaguars out here."

"That's a pleasant thought."

"The thing about jaguars is that they attack from above." He shined his light at the limbs before us. "They're excellent tree-climbers. They camp for hours, waiting for their prey. Then they pounce."

He spun around quickly, arms up, ready to defend himself. Nothing from the trees.

I asked if we couldn't please talk about something else.

"Not talking about the dangers won't make them disappear, Fr. Murphy. Old gods, big cats, do you really think your brother could survive out here?"

"I don't know. Stephen never struck me as much of a survivalist. Then again, there are a lot of things about my brother I don't know."

We hiked on for some time more. After thirty minutes or so, Tobit grabbed my shoulder.

"Look," he said.

I followed the beam of his flashlight to a large outcrop just above us. There sat a cabin, small and square, built into the side of the mountain.

"It almost looks new."

"It does."

"Do you think Stephen's inside?"

We approached slowly to find out. Though there were no lights inside the cabin, the place didn't look abandoned, for there was virtually no overgrowth on the roof or any of the walls. I ran my flashlight over the front of the building. No chimney. No windows, either. There was, however, a small flush door, on which I knocked three times.

No answer.

I knocked again. "Stephen? Stephen, are you in there? It's your brother."

Still no answer.

"Maybe he's out for the night," said Tobit.

"Doing what?"

He shrugged.

I knocked again, called out even louder, but still nothing. I tried the knob and found that the door was unlocked.

136

"Wait, Fr. Murphy, are you sure we should trespass?"

"Would you rather stay out here with the jaguars and ghosts?"

Tobit shook his head.

"Alright then."

It was warm inside and very dark. With no windows to let in the moon, our flashlights provided the only illumination, which wasn't much. I swept mine back and forth across the floorboards and quickly found that the place was a mess. Plastic water bottles littered the ground, as did empty cans of beans and vegetables and fruit cocktail. The air stank of tuna fish.

"Here," said Tobit, discovering a gas lamp in the corner of the room. When he turned it on, a soft, yellow brilliance washed over the space, revealing a table, chairs, various cooking supplies.

"Stephen? Hello? Stephen? Well, I guess that settles it," I said. "My brother really has gone and snapped. Is it just me, or is this place giving off a creepy doomsday-bunker kind of vibe?"

Tobit knelt to examine something on the floor.

"What's that?"

"I don't know," he said. "Be careful. It looks sharp."

I knelt down beside him. There were many reflective shards, as if a mirror had been shattered, only it wasn't glass.

"There's more," said Tobit. "A whole trail of them."

We followed the line of broken pieces to a bedroom just beyond the kitchen. It was darker here because the oil lamp was far away, and so we had to resort to our flashlights again to make sense of things. The trail ran past a cot, a pile of dirty sheets, and a greasy, yellow pillow, eventually ending at a large cardboard box. I removed the lid, revealing a horde of DVDs. All the cases had been ripped opened. All the discs had been smashed.

"Charles Darwin and the Religion of Death," Tobit read curiously. He looked up at me and asked why my brother would do something like this?

Before I could answer, there came a noise from the door. We both jumped.

A man was standing before us now, white-skinned and wild-looking, with muddy rags for clothes and a white-peppered beard curling from chin to chest. His eyes were small and sharp, like needle-points, and he carried a long hunting knife in one of his hands. In the other, he held a dead rabbit.

"Who are you?" said the man. "What are you doing here?" He dropped the rabbit and brandished his knife at us. There was fear in his eyes, that dangerous look of panic one sees in an animal cornered. "Get of here. This is my home. You don't belong."

I could hardly believe it. Though he looked more like one of those spear-wielding, mastodon-pelted Neanderthals than a former academic, this was undeniably...

"Stephen?" I said.

My brother titled his head at the invocation.

"Stephen, don't you recognize me? It's Leo. Leo Murphy."

A moment of tense silence. Tobit, who was occasionally an idiot, decided this was the appropriate moment to step forward and introduce himself. Stephen didn't take the hand that was offered him, but backed away slowly, stopping only to retrieve his rabbit.

"What the hell happened to you?" I said. "The last I heard, you were coming down to San Juandigo to do some humanitarian work. Now I talk to Dr. Mayrose, and she tells me you abandoned the project halfway through? Why are you living out here on this mountain? And why do you look like an insane person?"

My brother didn't answer me. Instead, he laid his dead rabbit on the table, cut its chest open with his hunting knife, and began pulling off the skin.

"Jesus, could you not?"

"How did you find me? Was it Kitty? Is she the one who sent you?"

"What? No. What are talking about? No one *sent* me. I came on my own volition. It was a guy named Bembé who told us you were up here. He said you'd gone crazy and bribed some desperate men to build you a cabin. I assumed he was exaggerating, but I guess not."

Stephen gave me a look out of the corner of his eye. He'd run into some trouble with the last bit of fur and had resorted to hacking the rabbit multiple times in the crotch. Once the skin was gone, he laid the pile of pink muscle on the table and began carving up the sections, removing the legs first and then separating the head from the torso.

"Looks delicious. When's dinner?"

"You aren't staying."

"For Christ's sake, of course I'm not staying. Will you look around? This place is a shithole."

The rabbit, once it was butchered, went into a big iron pot with some water and vegetables. Stephen had a portable gas burner for cooking. As I watched him prepare the stew, I wondered to myself whether I had missed something important while on vacation. Had there been a nuclear holocaust I wasn't aware of? Was this how people lived nowadays?

"If it wasn't Kitty who sent you, then why are you here?"

The question startled me.

Stephen glanced up from the pot and said, "You're a long way from Chippewa County."

"Yeah, and it's a long story, too."

He eyed me suspiciously.

"I'm on vacation, alright."

"You can't afford a vacation like this. Not unless the Church sent you. The Church didn't send you, did they?"

"No, the Church didn't send me. If you want to know the truth, the Church and I aren't exactly…"

139

"Aren't exactly what?"

"Well, the Church and I aren't exactly tight anymore. I'm no longer a priest in the traditional sense. I've been defrocked."

A look of surprise flashed across my brother's face as the trappings of madness momentarily left him. If only for an instant, we became Leo and Stephen again, the Murphy brothers, reuniting in the unlikeliest of places. While he stared at me over the now-bubbling pot of stew, I stared right back at him and knew that each of us was trying to make sense of the other. It was like coming across a passage of an ancient language you'd learned once long ago. Somewhere deep inside, the knowledge was still there, and if only we could summon it, then all the markings would lose their strangeness and become clear.

"I'm done with that business, too," said Stephen.

"What business?"

He waved his hand in a gesture of dismissal. "The Church. Religion. God. People. The world. All of it."

"Oh," I said.

He repeated himself: "All of it."

26

It wasn't true, what people said, that my brother's conversion from atheism to Christianity was inspired by the passing of our father, though I understood why everyone wanted to believe it. Dad was a man broken by the untimely death of his wife. To think that he might, through his own untimely death, have saved that son which he could only ever disappoint in living made for a nice story, only it wasn't true. I know this because on the day we buried our father, I learned many things about Stephen that seemed strange and incoherent at the time, but then made perfect sense a few months later when he resigned from the university, divorced Gertrude, and started giving crazy lectures about a 6,000 year-old Earth.

But I'm getting ahead of myself.

The funeral first.

It was a small, bleak gathering, few friends, fewer family. I didn't say the mass, though I did eulogize, which didn't go too well since I was in no mood to deliver the thing. Only a few days earlier, I'd received word that the happiest period of my life—my time spent at St. Raphael's—was coming to an end. I'd like to tell you it was some juicy scandal that got me exiled, but really it was just a numbers issue. St. Peter's needed a priest, St. Raphael's had one to spare, and so I ended up packing my bags and burying my father all in the same week.

Stephen and Gertrude hosted the after-funeral reception. We crammed into their tiny apartment, exchanged somber words, and ate horrible deli sandwiches provided by the catering company. If you want to know the truth, it was the food that tipped me off to something being wrong here. Whenever I'd visited previously, my brother and his wife had always made a point of serving delectable, albeit slightly pretentious fare. Smoked salmon, for example, or dehydrated vegetable chips. Brie and prosciutto crostini. Even when I'd met them during the throes of their tenure push—possibly the most strenuous period of the intellectual life—we'd dined on pita chips and humus and cubes of cantaloupe, sitting Indian-style around their circular coffee table. On one occasion, I remember none of us had his or her own plate, which meant there was a constant, complicated, and stress-inducing dance of hands over the three communal bowls. Whenever I grazed Gertrude's fingers, I swear I felt a chill run down my spine. About halfway through the meal, there was an awkward lull in conversation, so I asked how things were going at work. This was a sore subject, I soon realized. Without either one saying it explicitly, it became clear that while nothing was set in stone as of yet, it looked like Stephen was going to get tenure and Gertrude was not. This surprised me because Stephen—baggy-eyed, bone-thin, unshaven, etc.—looked like the one who was stressed out of his mind, but maybe that's just what it takes/the name of the game when it comes to academia. Gertrude, meanwhile, was showered, sweet-smelling, and strikingly beautiful as always. She was also going to be out on the street come spring, or worse, offered a year-by-year lectureship.

It was the algae's fault. That's how Stephen explained it. (Gertrude, I should note, was a very prideful woman and would never offer an excuse like this.) Her research involved a particular strand of algae which a few years back had shown promise as a potential bio-fuel. Unfortunately, this promise had not panned out, meaning that her work (while still good solid scientific research) was not nearly as sexy as it might've been.

"Hey," I said, honestly trying to find a silver lining, I swear, and definitely not rubbing it in, "remember what Edison said about inventing the light bulb."

Gertrude stared daggers at me across the coffee table. I think the bowl of hummus froze over. Stephen fumbled a pita-chip into the cantaloupe.

"Well," said Gertrude, straining to hold back her venom, "Edison never went up for tenure, though, did he?"

"Coleslaw, Leo?"

"Thank you, Aunt Mary."

"I wanted to pass along my condolences."

"I appreciate it very much."

"That's your brother's wife, isn't it, standing alone in the kitchen?"

"Hm? Oh yes, that's Gertrude."

"Beautiful woman, isn't she?"

"Yes, quite beautiful."

"And smart, too, just like Stephen. I can see why they fell for each other. Is she a professor as well?"

Shoveling a too-rich helping of artichoke dip onto my plate, I explained to Aunt Mary as softly as I could that Gertrude had unfortunately not received tenure and was now exploring her options in the private sector.

"Oh, I see."

"It's a touchy subject. Best not to bring it up."

"I'll add her to my prayer list."

Aunt Mary gave me a tender squeeze on the arm and then went off to find my brother. I remained at the coffee table, staring over the mountain of mini Reuben at Stephen's wife. It was not like Gertrude to be so outwardly aloof. At parties, she was usually the perfect hostess: engaging, intelligent, talkative but not domineering, always quick to season an introduction with a factoid of mutual interest, even though afterwards, I'm

143

sure she spoke critically of each guest in turn. Presently, she was drinking wine beside the dishwasher. The bottle stood next to her, almost empty. No doubt the funeral had made her uncomfortable. It was a stereotypically Catholic affair: plenty of gloomy hymns, etc. I wondered briefly whether atheists had more trouble coping with death than the rest of us, and then thought probably not since technically it was believers who had to rationalize this whole thing in light of an allegedly benevolent God.

"Are you feeling okay, Gertrude?"

"Leo, I'm so sorry for your loss."

She hugged me quickly, firmly, desperately. It was not what I'd expected given our chilly past. All I could say was, "Thanks."

"Do you want something to drink?" She gestured to the wine bottle and then realized with a flash of embarrassment that it was nearly empty. "Oh, I—"

"It's fine," I told her. "I'll just have a coke."

I retrieved it from the refrigerator myself. When I turned back, Gertrude was staring at me and also standing closer than was normal. I retreated slowly.

"Maybe you should lie down. It's been a tough day for all of us."

"Oh, not for Stephen."

I raised my eyebrows. It wasn't just the words but the way she'd spoken them that was strange. Like laughing almost, or forced singing. She smiled without any joy in her expression at all. Then she really did laugh, which was even stranger.

"He's got it all figured out, you know. Things like this don't bother him anymore. Must be nice, don't you think?" She paused long enough that I couldn't tell whether the question was rhetorical. "Did you try the potato salad?"

I told her no, I hadn't yet.

"Don't bother. It's pedestrian." She took a long drink from her wine.

"Are you sure you're feeling okay?"

"Of course," she said. "Never better. Well, considering." She nodded to the black-trimmed crowd assembled in her living room. Then her eyes got very wide, and she stepped towards me again, pulling me into a sort of tipsy half-hug that wasn't so much friendly as inappropriate. "Can I tell you something personal, Leo?"

"Maybe I should get Stephen."

"No, don't do that. It's about him. Oops, I mean us. It's about *us*." Suddenly her tone became very formal, and her whole body stiffened in mock propriety. "Henceforth, we are to speak only in the third person, like royalty, for kings and queens never have marital problems. They are linguistically superior, you understand." She laughed again in that mirthless, discomforting way.

"Gertrude?"

"We're seeing a therapist," she whispered.

"Oh," I said. I didn't know what else to say. Attempting to conjure an appropriate reply, all I could think about was how we were still locked together in whatever you would call this partial embrace.

"Don't tell Stephen I told you."

"Of course."

"It's supposed to be a private matter."

"I understand."

"Do you, Leo?"

She stared at me now with such intensity, and her grip was so tight around my shoulder, that I was suddenly afraid, not for her, but for me. I felt like a man who dives into the water with the notion of saving someone, but then ends up drowning himself.

The fear in my eyes must've sobered her, for Gertrude loosened her grip and spun away.

"I should've had an affair," she announced from the sink.

The words weren't whispered, but I believe they passed unnoticed by the congregation in general. We were separated, the two of us, partitioned off into the kitchen, and anyway, she'd turned on the faucet, which always made a racket because of the old pipes.

"I didn't," she clarified.

She took the wine bottle and turned it over the sink. I watched the dregs spill out into the flowing water, dark red disappearing into transparency. When it was empty, she turned the bottle back over, filled it partway, emptied it again, and then placed it in a grocery bag next to the dishwasher. There it clinked against empty olive jars and other glassware waiting to be recycled.

"I didn't," she repeated, "but I should've."

27

The rabbit actually wasn't that bad. Gamey? Sure. Stringy? You bet. But the broth was nice, and the vegetables pleasant enough, and since Stephen only had the one bowl, Tobit and I ate straight from the pot, passing the ladle back and forth between us, slurping like a couple of philistines. My brother, meanwhile, eyed us distrustfully from the head of the table. He'd finished his portion ages ago and now just sat there, not saying much. About halfway through the meal, I'd asked him how his other projects were going.

"The peanut butter thing. What's new with the peanut butter thing?"

"Not peanut butter," he said.

"No?"

"It's crickets now. Entomophagy: the next big breakthrough in global nutrition." When I gave him a dubious look, he added condescendingly, "Insects are an efficient source of protein. Certain species of crickets can be bred by the millions at low cost."

"Really?" said Tobit. "And that's safe?" He glanced at the stew, giving the ladle a suspicious stir. "I don't know if I would ever *willingly* eat a bug."

"If you're hungry enough," said Stephen, "you'll eat anything."

So yeah, not exactly the best dinner table conversation.

The longer I sat there, the more fed up I got with my brother's whole doomsday-hermit charade. It was just like Stephen to pull this kind of shit. I mean seriously, did he have to go and one-up me every chance he got? Couldn't he just let me have my little midlife crisis? Why make a caricature out of it? Look at that ridiculous beard. And those fingernails!

"So what was it, huh? You weren't touching little boys, were you?"

I glanced up from the stew. "Excuse me?"

"I never had you pegged for a pedophile, but I guess we don't really know each other all that well, do we?"

"I'm not a pedophile," I assured my brother. "If you don't believe me, ask my choir director."

"Ah," said Stephen, nodding his head. "So it wasn't little boys, but it *was* your cock that did you in. Well, I hope she was worth it."

"Don't talk that way about Ms. Campbell," said Tobit.

My brother smiled at him. "Why? Is she your mother?"

"Jesus, it's nothing like that. The kid's never even met her. He certainly isn't my son. But Charley's not just a fling," I added. "I really do love her. And anyway, she wasn't the reason I got defrocked. They kicked me out because of an essay."

"No shit? An essay?"

I nodded.

"Well, what did you write?" said Stephen. "It must've been pretty juicy."

Actually it wasn't, now that I thought about it. Aside from the imprudent passage condoning the crucifixion of Jesus, the majority of the piece was objective and thoughtful, maybe even a little boring. It's hard to write gripping theology for a general audience. No one likes slogging through page after page of dense Christology.

"It's not important," I told Stephen.

148

"Like hell it isn't."

"Honestly, it's inside baseball. I quote dusty theologians and centuries-old dogma. It's really not the kind of thing you'd be interested in."

He glared at me.

"What?"

"You don't think I'm smart enough, do you?"

"Jesus. It isn't that. You said yourself you're done with religion. Quote: 'I'm done with that business. The Church. God. People. All of it.'"

"And you think I'm being ridiculous."

"Well, I certainly don't think you're being responsible. Those shattered DVDs? I could care less about those. In fact, I think it's good you've finally given up that creationism nonsense. But abandoning your charity work and running off to this mountain like some kind of crazy person? Haven't you thought about your wife? Your children? How could you leave them behind?"

"I don't know. Didn't you leave Charley behind?"

That shut me up alright. Granted, our situations were entirely different. I'd begged Charley to run away with me, while Stephen hadn't even left Kitty a note. And it wasn't like I was going to spend my whole life in San Juandigo. As soon as I had things figured out, it was back to Chippewa County to win over the woman I loved.

"Maybe you *should* tell him," said Tobit, giving me one of those don't-blame-me-for-this kind of shrugs. "He is your brother, you know, and we did track him down specifically so you two could make up."

"Ha!" said Stephen. "Leo extending the olive branch? Don't hold your breath. Did you know we've sent him Christmas cards for more than ten years, and not once did he pick up the phone to thank us?"

"But he's different now. You are different now, aren't you, Fr. Murphy?"

I stared at Tobit for a few moments before letting out a deep sigh. To be entirely honest, I was embarrassed about my essay. Now that I'd had some distance from it, the piece seemed juvenile and maybe even a bit whiny. So what if I wasn't happy at St. Peter's? There were plenty of folks living unhappy lives, and none of them had shaken their fist at God. Where did I get off anyway? Leo Murphy: what a joke. I couldn't even sit through a damn finance meeting without turning it into some kind of existential crisis. My brother, by contrast, had seen some real shit. Kids starving to death in the streets. Malaria. Ebola. Etc. Those were things that could justifiably keep you up at night. Meanwhile, why was I so upset again? Because I had to live in the suburbs? Because I had to preach to rich people? Talk about the banality of suffering.

"Well?" said Stephen.

I turned to him and said, "It was on the Paschal Mystery. I asked why Jesus needed to die for our sins. Why didn't God just forgive us without sacrificing his son?"

He though a moment. "And they threw you out because of this?"

"Well, it was mainly my conclusion that the bishops took exception to."

"Which was?"

"Basically that Jesus deserved to be crucified. You know, kind of a payback thing."

There was a moment of silence, and then my brother started laughing. Actually, I started laughing, too. I guess the whole thing was sort of funny in a way.

28

Dear Charley,

You'll never guess where I'm writing this or who's sitting next to me or what all has transpired in the last few days to send me hurtling back to you at 500+ mph. First things first: my vacation is over. That's right, I've left San Juandigo behind and with it the *Felicity*, which is still docked at harbor and not scheduled to depart for another six weeks. Currently, I'm on route to Tucson International Airport via Houston and then Dallas/Fort Worth. We're headed into the desert like the Israelites in search of the Promised Land. Who, you ask, is accompanying me? Well, there's Tobit Portnoy for one. It's his girlfriend we're after, that Madonna Garfield chick who butchered his father's cow and then fed it to him and then left for the University of Arizona and hasn't been heard from since. Our primary objective is a reconciliation of the romantic variety. In fact, we have three such reconciliations planned, but I'll get to all that later.

Before I go on, I must tell you that Stephen Murphy is traveling with us. Yes, you read that correctly. Stephen, my younger brother, with whom I've been estranged for God knows how many years, has reentered my life with providential timing. He's suffered some kind of spiritual breakdown recently, leaving him a shell of his former self. Tobit and I

151

discovered him living like a hermit on a mountain in San Juandigo where he had fled from his wife and children and has clearly lost whatever religious certainty that once led him to produce so many best-selling DVDs. I must say that despite his long fingernails and crazy-person beard, I like him much better now. He isn't nearly as condescending as before, and he no longer makes me sick with envy since his life has fallen apart. As I write these words, he's perusing a SkyMall catalogue while sipping a ginger ale on ice. I couldn't conceive a more unpretentious portrait.

The second reconciliation—as you might suspect—will be between Stephen and his wife, Kitty, whom you'll recall sells religiously-themed birthday cakes over the internet. Honestly, I don't know what will happen when my brother returns home after we finish this business with Tobit and Madonna, though I have my fingers crossed for a prodigal son scenario in which the fattened calf is slaughtered and all is forgiven. Admittedly, this hope is not entirely unselfish. It does not escape me that Stephen is not the only Murphy presently estranged from his beloved, and yes, Charley, you've guessed it: the third reconciliation will be ours. After my pit stops in Tucson and Savannah, I mean to return to Chippewa County and win your heart.

What inspires such confidence?

Well, I used the wrong word earlier when I told you my vacation was over. I should've written *pilgrimage*, for it truly has been a spiritual journey, these last few months, and I mean that in all sincerity and good faith. But you will counter, "Leo, you haven't gone to Jerusalem or Fatima or partaken of the waters at Lourdes. All you did was sail around the Caribbean for a couple of weeks and then relax at a tropical resort," which may be technically accurate, I admit, but a summary like that disregards myriad psychic and emotional breakthroughs which have led me to develop an entirely new outlook on life. In short, I'm a changed man, Charley. When I left you, I was broken and unhappy. Presently, I'm healed and full of hope.

Affectionately yours,

Leo

29

"Basically it's because you all struck me as very Zen individuals," said Kiki Masterson over her steaming cup of chai tea. She offered to pop another three mugs into the microwave, but Tobit, Stephen, and I all politely declined. Kiki smiled at us and then sat down at her desk. Her study-space was arranged quite mindfully. Laptop and mechanical pencils lay perfectly perpendicular to a stack of Comparative Religion textbooks, next to which sat a fat golden Buddha. On the other side rested a miniature sand garden carefully raked into a design most suitable for meditation. There was even a tiny bonsai tree sprouting from one corner of the box.

"Regardless," said Stephen, making sure to keep plenty of distance between himself and this freshman coed, "you probably shouldn't make it a habit of opening your door to strangers."

At least not strangers who look like the three of us, he might've added.

But Kiki just sipped her tea and continued to smile from across the dorm room. She explained that she was usually very beholden to AU residential policies, but in this instance, she decided to make an exception since we'd mentioned her roommate—make that *ex*-roommate—Madonna Garfield.

"The truth is, I'm worried about her," Kiki confessed, though her face registered no sign of this emotion. "Okay, I'll admit it. First semester, we weren't exactly best friends. There were some rough patches along the way. If I'm being honest, that night she played the *Sex Pistols* album over and over and refused to put on headphones even though she knew I had my Western Civ final at eight o'clock the next morning…but, you know, it's like what the Buddha said. 'Holding onto anger is like grasping a hot coal with the intent of throwing it at someone. You're the one who ends up getting burned.'"

"Very wise," said Tobit with a thoughtful nod.

Not nearly so impressed, I gave Kiki a dubious looking-over. She was awfully tan for a human being, not orange like you see from one of those UV cancer pods, but bronze, almost brown, and with hair so blonde it could've been white. She wore open-toed sandals made from what I assumed to be imitation leather, and her dress—pink like a cactus rose—was about as flimsy as an undergraduate's grasp of Heidegger.

"I can tell you're really committed to this whole Buddhism shtick," I said.

She answered yes, absolutely, one hundred percent committed. In fact, she'd been practicing her meditation all year and was actually getting pretty good at it.

"You may not believe me, but sometimes I can go literally *hours* without a single thought in my head."

"You don't say?"

"Be nice," said Stephen from the corner.

Tobit, meanwhile, was making a careful study of the left half of Kiki's dorm, which was currently unoccupied unless you counted the empty desk and the lumpy twin mattress stripped of its sheets. On the wall at various locations, scabs of glue residue marked the spots where non-regulation duct tape had been used to hang posters. An ominous black stain rain the length of carpet from window to AC unit.

"That's from burning gunpowder," said Kiki nonchalantly as if announcing it were hot today or that she was thinking about going for a walk later.

Tobit looked up from the floor and said, "Burning what now?"

"It was for a poem. William had this image in mind and wanted to make sure it was accurate." Kiki pointed out the smoke detector on the ceiling, which I hadn't noticed was disconnected, and said that he and Madonna had conducted this experiment with the help of a Sophomore Chemistry major while she was away pulling an all-nighter at the library.

"How considerate of them."

Kiki shrugged. "Holding onto anger is grasping a hot coal."

Tobit said, "Wait a minute. Back up a second. Who's William?"

"Sorry?"

"William. You mentioned a William?"

"Oh, right. William Weatherfield. Well, *Prince William* is what a lot of girls call him. Very dreamy English gentleman type. Talks like this. Parents are from Oxford or Cambridge or one of those. He's Madonna's boyfriend."

For all her Buddhists pretenses, Kiki showed no qualms in conveying this soul-crushing piece of information, the delivery of which elicited a strange, guttural, choking sound from Tobit and caused him to collapse upon Madonna's bed as if shot through the neck.

"Oh, Jesus," I said, kneeling at the kid's side. When I grasped his hand, I found that his palm was trembling and slick with sweat. His face had turned ghost white, and he was looking up at me, eyes wide, lips trembling.

"Is he drunk?" asked Kiki. "Should I call Health Services?"

I told her not to be an idiot. He wasn't drunk. He was heartbroken. Couldn't she put two and two together?

"Sorry?"

"This is Madonna's boyfriend!" I snapped. "Or ex-boyfriend, I suppose. He's been writing her emails and trying to call her all year. You might've been more tactful with that William Weatherfield bombshell."

"Oh," said Kiki, who then stared silently at her golden Buddha.

Stephen told her not to worry. She couldn't have known.

Tobit cried out, "I should've known! I should've known!" and began writhing atop the mattress that Madonna and William (I didn't have the heart to point this out) had probably fooled around on some time or another.

"You were right, Fr. Murphy. I've been a fool for so long. Why didn't I see things clearly? Obviously she didn't love me. Did she ever love me? I've been such a fool. It was stupid of us to come here."

While Tobit sobbed, Kiki glanced around the room uncomfortably. I could tell by her face that she now regretted violating AU residential policies. Better to have left these three wackos outside in the blazing Arizona heat and let campus security deal with them. I got up and stood next to her.

"Look," I said. "My brother's right. It isn't your fault. We shouldn't go around killing the messenger, especially when that messenger has had a hard enough go of it already. But you have to understand that we've come a very long way to find Madonna, and what you just told us is from Tobit's perspective kind of a dagger to the crotch, emotionally speaking. Anyway, we need more details. This William thing, is it serious? How long has it been going on? Does it have anything to do with why Madonna doesn't live here anymore?"

Before Kiki could answer, Stephen put his hand on my shoulder and said, "Do you think this is a good idea, Leo?" He nodded to Tobit, who was no longer sobbing but still weeping quietly, his face buried in a pillow with no pillowcase. "Maybe we should just get out of here. Let sleeping dogs lie."

"I agree," said Kiki. "The Buddha teaches that suffering is caused by desire. Consider the second noble truth. If we wish others to conform to our expectations—"

"Just save it," I told her. "And that goes for you too," I said to Stephen. "You guys, this isn't the time for noble truths or nirvana or any of that bullshit. Don't you see who we are? We're Odysseus come back to Ithaca. Now let's go string our bows and slaughter some suitors."

I slapped Tobit hard upon the shoulder and told him to sit up already. He's wasn't going to win back Madonna's heart blubbering like a little kid.

Stephen pointed out that in Homer's version, Penelope had remained eternally faithful, which was something we should consider in this case.

"Where are they?" I said to Kiki, ignoring my brother's admonition. "Madonna and William. Are they staying at his dorm? Are they out at some party?"

The girl looked down at her Buddha again and said, "Um… I don't know if I should tell you."

"Why? Because of that suitor-slaughtering comment? Listen, don't worry about that. It won't come to blows or anything. Jesus, we're all adults here. I just want to give my friend a chance. Look at him. Doesn't he deserve a chance?"

Actually, it was hard to say what Tobit deserved at this juncture. Though no longer weeping into Madonna's pillow, he still hadn't achieved verticality, but was rocking back and forth in the fetal position, knees pressed against his stomach, shins cupped in his massive hands. At regular intervals, a new wave of sadness would pass through him, causing his muscles to spasm as if exposed to an electrical current.

"I knew this was going to happen," said Stephen.

"Shut up. You aren't being helpful."

"I'm not being cruel, either. Just realistic."

"He's right," muttered Tobit. "Let's just give up, Fr. Murphy. You were right. From the very beginning, you told me this was all a fantasy, and look, you were right."

At these words, a heavy silence fell over Kiki Masterson's dorm as if all the air had been sucked out via a giant vacuum. I sat down on the edge of Madonna's bed and patted Tobit gingerly upon his Achilles.

"We aren't giving up," I told him. "Not now. Not this easily. If Madonna won't take you back, then where does that leave me and my brother, huh? Now come on. Get up. Pull yourself together. And you, Ms. Dali Lama, I believe I asked you a question."

Kiki smiled nervously.

"What's wrong? I thought we were all Zen individuals?"

"Not really," she said. "But…well, in all honesty…" She cast a furtive glance to her Buddha and spoke the next words in barely a whisper. "In all honesty, I don't much care for William. Even if he is English and charming and a brilliant poet, he still burnt my carpet, which is going to come out of *my* security deposit, and he's been a very bad influence on my roommate. If you want to find him, he's probably over at the Modern Languages building. There's a symposium there tonight, kind of an open mic thing for undergraduates. Oh, and Father?" Kiki took one last sip from her chai tea and then winked at me through the steam. "I hope your friend kicks his ass."

30

William Weatherfield was a legend at the University of Arizona. Handsome, insightful, charming, absurdly productive, the young man far exceeded the allure normally allotted to international students and seemed to exist on an entirely different plane, one usually reserved for gods, not mortals. At least this was the impression we got from his fellow undergraduates. In the six blocks between Kiki's dormitory and the Modern Languages building, we managed to survey three separate gaggles of coeds (all of whom were heading to that night's reading), and each girl made it clear that to understand Weatherfield, we first needed to know about his roommate, Prince Ramesh Aggarwal, originally from India. The two men had met at Oxford some years ago. At that time Ramesh was working towards a degree in economics and renting a room in the house of a kindly old widow named Mrs. Humble, whose late husband, George, had been a diplomat and also a good friend of Ramesh's grandfather. Ramesh was a wonderful tenant. He was studious and fiercely intelligent, and he loved Mrs. Humble's cooking. Often, he devoured whole plates of scotch eggs, deep bowls of steak and kidney pie, drank endless pots of tea. He even had a taste for disgusting things like haggis and black pudding. Whenever they shared a meal, Mrs. Humble would look on with a mix of pride and admiration. Her late husband would've celebrated such an exhibition, for according to George, a good appetite was imperative in a young man. It suggested strength and readiness and (more vaguely) a certain spiritual hunger one often sees in persons of significance.

Such was the pleasure Mrs. Humble took in Ramesh's company that a few months into the term, when an unforeseen complication regarding George's pension left her unexpectedly strapped, she did not hesitate for a moment in placing an ad in the local paper.

"Room for Rent: fully furnished, private bath, walking distance from Oxford University."

The price, address, and contact information were all provided, and the last line read, "Cultured individuals preferred."

Enter William Weatherfield.

Age: 25. Height: 5' 10'' Weight: 160 lbs. Complexion: fair. Occupation: none. Marital Status: eternal servant of the cruel mistress, Poetry.

Weatherfield was currently (and had been for the past four and a half years) deep in labor on a composition of epic verse. The poem was titled *Poorman's Progress* and concerned the Industrial Revolution, specifically the plight of one Everyman Poorman, a dubiously-named papersmith forced to foreclose on his humble shop thanks to the invention of the Fourdrinier Machine. The entire project was just awful, not that it mattered, for at this point in his life, Weatherfield obviously didn't care about poetry so much as being a poet. To put it bluntly, he was extremely lazy and yet very popular with the ladies. Girls loved his waifish, bohemian body, his scraggly half-beard, the way he *felt* things such that the word required italicization. His room was genius small and cramped with thick books and messy stacks of paper. It also smelled odiously of clove cigarettes even though smoking was strictly forbidden via Mrs. Humble's ad. (The old woman, it must be admitted, was as hopelessly taken with "cultured" Weatherfield as the long parade of women who now frequented her late husband's study.)

Most days, Weatherfield rose at 10:30, about two hours after the previous night's conquest had departed. He would stumble downstairs, prepare himself a strong cup of tea, nibble a pastry or two, wander aimlessly to the living room, take up residence on the chesterfield, switch on the tele, scribble vaguely in his notebook, and watch four episodes of *Dr. Who*. If Mrs. Humble happened to be around, he would smile at her and say very insightful things about the episode. She would blush, of course. Then, to show that she, too, was cultured and invested in the arts, she would ask how his poem was coming.

"Oh Mrs. Humble, I feel as if the top of my head is taken off."

"Oh dear. Well, I hope you aren't straining too hard."

Like everyone else, Prince Aggarwal was taken with the new tenant, though for completely different reasons. "I must say, Weatherfield, I truly admire you," he announced one Sunday afternoon when the poet finally emerged from bed.

"How's that?" asked William with a sleepy smile.

Ramesh set aside his copy of Adam Smith's *Wealth of Nations* and passed his suitemate a leftover scone and the jar of blackberry jam. Then he said with sincere admiration that was in no way tinged with scorn, "Somehow you live the life of a king on the salary of a peasant."

Weatherfield laughed at this, for it was true he had but little money.

"You must teach me your secret," said the prince quite earnestly.

"No. First I must take issue with your premise. The peasant part, I accept, but the life of a king?" William spread a generous amount of jam on his scone, for amongst his many vices, he possessed a notorious sweet tooth. Speaking softly now just in case Mrs. Humble was snooping: "Listen, Ramesh,

162

I love it here as much as you do, but would someone like Solomon ever stoop to rent my room?"

"Yes, if his wisdom were not hyperbole."

"I don't believe you."

"But it's true," said the prince, "for a wise man could want nothing more than to maximize pleasure and avoid pain, and in this regard, you are a worthy rival of Solomon."

Weatherfield laughed again and then took a very large bite of his scone. He was rather fond of Ramesh. He enjoyed that he could carry on a joke. "Very well," he said, "I admit that my life has its comforts, but Solomon, I think, had 700 wives and 300 concubines."

"That's correct."

"And my personal statistics are not nearly so impressive."

"Don't fret," said the prince. "You'll get there eventually. Just last week, you slept with four women in three nights. If one were to extrapolate those numbers—and I'm assuming you want nothing to do with marriage, per se, so 'sexual partner' shall stand in for wife—then it will only take a few years for you to equal and then surpass the ancient king of legend."

Weatherfield looked up from his scone. He wondered whether this poker-faced scholar was having some fun with him. "You think I'm a man-slag, don't you, Ramesh? Well, sucks to you and your uptight culture. I won't renounce my dalliances. Those women, far from being concubines, were willing and then satisfied, and anyway, a poet requires a certain number of affairs. Not carnally, mind you, but spiritually. There's a sense of nourishment involved. A renewal. In short, I get more from these women than a good shag."

"Oh, I won't argue that point," said the prince. "I admit, I've only been observing you for a short time, but the girls you encounter seem to provide much more than sexual favors. Tiffany, for example, gave you a lift to the liquor shop the other day. That must've been quite useful since you don't own an auto. Also, Rachel, and I hope you don't mind my snooping, lent you two hundred pounds to cover last month's rent."

"How the hell did you—" Weatherfield bristled and then restrained himself. It was all good fun for Ramesh to be teasing him, but what the young chap didn't understand was that the life of the artist, since it came with particular burdens, also allowed for particular liberties.

"Then there was Emily who was always giving away—"

"Okay, okay, you've made your point," William said, laughing off the slights. "I'm a rogue and a mooch, I won't deny it. But honestly now, all my transgressions are venial when one considers the god of my ambitions. Poetry, Ramesh! She is my true master."

The prince smiled uneasily, but said nothing.

"You disagree?"

"Well, it's just that I never actually see you *writing* poetry. Granted, I'm away at class most of the day so…"

"Yes, and I was just going to say that," snapped Weatherfield. "Always away at class, so how would you even know? And anyway, poetry isn't like ditch-digging or accounting. The progress isn't so easily measured. Some days I labor and labor and yet produce nothing more than a single line. Other days, the words fly from my pen as if I'd dreamed them all the night before."

"Do you often dream of poetry?" asked Ramesh.

William eyed him over his half-finished scone. He couldn't tell if the question suggested earnest curiosity or sarcasm. "Not as much as I would like perhaps, but such are the ways of the Muse. Her visits are blissful but not frequent."

"In that regard, she is not like your other lady friends at all. I mean the frequency part," added Ramesh. "Blissfulness you've accomplished, or so I assume. I can only go by what I hear through the walls."

A few minutes ago, Weatherfield would've grinned at this comment. Now he just stared coldly. "There you go again, trying to shame me."

"Not in the least."

"I don't go around poking fun at your culture, so I would appreciate—"

"William, you misunderstand. In no way do I mean to criticize. Quite the opposite. I think your life is marvelous."

"For Christ's sake," said the poet, "it's not all shagging and sleeping-in. You sound just like my dad. He doesn't understand me either. Do you think I wanted to be working on my poem this long? No, it was supposed to be finished by now. I was to give readings in all the famous bookshops of London. Intelligent strangers were to laud me. Beautiful women were to call me genius."

"But beautiful women do call you genius, or at least Tiffany did."

"I don't care about Tiffany," shouted Weatherfield, pounding a fist upon Mrs. Humble's kitchen table. "I told you, Poetry is my god. Everything else, I'd just as soon be rid of."

"No, you couldn't do that. You'd be giving up too much."

Weatherfield glared at the prince over the open jar of blackberry jam. He had finally lost his patience. Ramesh wasn't some curious kind-hearted foreigner, he decided, but a snake in the brush just waiting to snap at his ankles.

"I'm tired of talking about this. I'm going to watch *Dr. Who*."

"Wait, William, please don't leave. I apologize if I've spoken rudely. It wasn't my intention to offend." Ramesh followed the poet into the living room and then put himself between the chesterfield and the tele so that he could not be ignored. "The thing is I'm worried about you. You're the happiest man in Britain, only you don't know it."

"Kindly remove yourself, Ramesh."

The prince didn't budge.

165

"I say, you can get on your magic carpet now and fly back to India."

"Not until I teach you something for your own sake. You need to give up these silly notions about poetry and suffering—"

"Silly?"

"—and I think I know how you can do it."

Weatherfield rolled his eyes. "Fine, if it'll shut you up. Go on and enlighten me."

"I propose a bet," said Ramesh.

"Jesus, this'll be rich. What are the stakes?"

"No less than our very lives."

"Ha! Okay. And the terms?"

The prince sat down on the chesterfield next to the poet. He spoke slowly and in a grave tone of voice as if the wager he was proposing were not merely a throwaway joke between friends but a contract of upmost seriousness.

"Listen," he said, "you say it's poetry that makes you happy, and I say it's all the other things, so let's settle this like proper scientists. I propose you live one year under extreme conditions. I'm not talking about anything dangerous. You needn't starve yourself or go without water or anything like that, but there are certain comforts you could safely forgo. These will be our variables."

Weatherfield looked at him suspiciously. "What do you mean, Ramesh? Enough of this preamble. Give me the specifics."

"Yes, of course, the specifics. The bet will last one year starting today. From this afternoon forward, you William Weatherfield, will give up all earthly pleasures not directly related to your personal safety. These pleasures include, but are not limited to, intercourse with random women, snogging or flirting or eliciting praise from these women, all television excluding emergency bulletins, Mrs. Humble's glorious cooking. (Don't worry. I shall provide you with a blander form

166

of sustenance.) You will also do without alcohol and cigarettes. Marijuana will be banned unless you can convince me that it is necessary for your work. All other recreational drugs must be gotten rid of, of course."

"What is this, a wager or an intervention?"

"You will rise at a decent hour," said Ramesh, pushing forward. "Let's say six on weekdays. On Sunday you may sleep until seven. If you need caffeine to function in the morning, I'll allow a single cup of strong black coffee or a spot of tea. After a modest breakfast, you'll spend your morning writing poetry. I'll check your progress when I return home between classes. I suggest you keep two notebooks from now on. In one you shall write your poetry. In the other, you shall write all your notes and outlines concerning that poetry. I agree that artistic progress is harder to measure than the fruits of other disciplines, but it is not impossible to measure. Let's set some parameters. A good day of work—and indeed, I expect most of your days will be good days, devoid as they are of distractions—a good day will consist of either one hundred lines of verse or five full pages of notes or some combination therein."

"Christ," said Weatherfield, "I'd be more prolific than Shakespeare at that rate."

"All the better," said the prince. "If Poetry be your god, then serve Her furiously. After lunch, you may have an hour's recreation. You may go for a walk or read for pleasure. If Mrs. Humble is about, you may partake in pleasant conversation. You may not, however, watch television."

"What's all this about television? What the hell's wrong with television?"

"Your afternoons shall be spent either in further composition and note-taking or revision of that morning's work. The same goes for your evenings."

"And when may I use the pisser, warden, or is that one of your unnecessary comforts?"

The prince only smiled. "Bodily needs may be administered to at your discretion. You will, however, obey a curfew. Lights out at ten o'clock. This will provide plenty of sleep, for good work requires good rest, and good work is what will bring you happiness, if we are to believe your assertions."

Despite feeling pricked, Weatherfield still might've laughed this whole business aside if it weren't for the pains Ramesh was taking in the particulars. As it was, he behaved as most children do when confronted with their own absurdity. He ignored all inconvenient evidence and dug in more staunchly.

"You said this bet will last a year, Ramesh. At the end of that year, how will we decide who's won?"

"Simple," said the prince. "If you keep the schedule I set for you, and by that I mean not only the writing of poetry but also the abstaining from all lesser pleasures, then you will be declared the victor."

"And what shall I win?"

"You mean besides the year of transcendental bliss?"

"Yes, of course, what do I get besides that?"

"A disciple," said Ramesh.

Weatherfield looked puzzled.

"I told you that the stakes were no less than our very lives. Therefore, if you prove correct in your assertion that happiness can be attained most abundantly through the service of the Muse, I shall quit my studies, give away all my possessions, renounce earthly pleasures, and dedicate my hours to the creation of verse. In short, William, I shall follow your lead. Now isn't that a prize worth attaining?"

Even a casual observer (and by that I imagine someone with one eye on the conversation and one eye on *Dr. Who*) could see that this prize was very disappointing. Regardless, what could Weatherfield say now? The sneaky Indian had backed him into a corner.

"But if I win," continued the prince, "then you will become my disciple."

168

"Meaning?"

"No more poetry. No more talk of suffering. That's all, really. I don't require much, especially not from someone already so well-versed in the consumption of delights."

"Enough," said William, getting angry again. "Stop talking to me like I'm some kind of libertine."

Weatherfield burned with ire. He'd been vilified and slandered and had suffered enough insults at the tongue of Ramesh the Philistine. All this he said and more in a very stirring speech, which I will omit here, for as Defense of Poesy's go, it was no Sir Philip Sidney. The conclusion, however, was just this: "I accept your wager, Ramesh. Bring me my pen."

31

"Hold on," I said. "You're telling me Weatherfield actually won this crazy bet?"

"That's right, Father."

"But how's that possible? The guy you've described couldn't have lasted a week under those conditions. I mean, no offense, but he sounds like a real jerkoff."

We were standing in the back of the atrium of the Modern Languages building, waiting for the reading to start. While I made a thorough investigation of the hors d'oeuvres table, the four girls with whom I was chatting all cast critical glances at my plate. I admit it was loaded down with more fruit, crackers, and fancy cheeses than socially appropriate, but what could I say? Paradise Cruise Lines had instilled in me a taste for the finer things.

"That was the old William," they insisted.

"He's changed now."

"Reformed."

"Born again."

"He's a completely new man."

"He doesn't care about things like sex and drugs anymore."

"*Earthly* desires."

"Pleasures of the *flesh*."

"*Opulence*."

"*Gaudiness.*"

I bit the fat, ripe teat of a chocolate-covered strawberry, defiant in my indulgence. I was none-too-pleased with the looks I was getting from these Weatherfield groupies, and I didn't appreciate their Protestant tone.

"He couldn't be entirely disinterested. Isn't he dating Madonna Garfield?"

The girls all bristled simultaneously.

"And from what I've heard—"

"She's nothing," they cut me off.

"Less than nothing."

"Just a little freak-show freshman."

"A head case."

"A *charity* case."

"The only reason William even lets her hang around is because he feels sorry for her."

"She has no other friends."

"And why would she? Have you seen what she looks like?"

"Or how she dresses?"

"My God, have you heard about her stories?"

"They're so...*disturbing.*"

I chewed another chocolate-covered strawberry and then placed the leafy crown beside a wedge of Gouda I planned on enjoying later. So much for Mr. Garfield's assertion that some time in the desert would do his daughter good. Socially, this place was about as welcoming as a tank of piranhas, or worse, because at least piranhas spare the bones. For obvious reasons, I was no big Madonna supporter either, but even I didn't think she deserved this kind of public stoning. I glanced around the room to see if Tobit had managed to find her yet. The atrium was large and packed with people, professors and undergraduates alike. Up at the front was a wide stage with a podium at the center, then about fifty rows of chairs, all filled.

Tobit, who'd abandoned me and Stephen the moment we stepped inside, was hurrying through the crowd, searching madly for his lost love. My brother, meanwhile, had taken up residence under a cork bulletin board just a few feet from the hors d'oeuvres table. The board was shaggy with multi-colored fliers advertising things like study groups and new clubs.

"Uh, Leo, you're gonna want to take a look at this."

"Huh?"

"Seriously," he said, ripping one of the pages from the board.

I excused myself from Weatherfield's fan club to examine the flier. It was a bright purple sheet with the words, "UA DRAMA DEPARTMENT" in bold across the top. At first, I didn't understand the significance of the literature—what did I care about some cultural enrichment trip to New York?—but when I saw Charley's black-and-white photo staring up at me from the page, I nearly dropped my plate.

"Did you know about this?" said Stephen.

"Did I—what do you mean, did I know?"

"You've been emailing her, haven't you?"

"Sending emails, yes. Receiving them, no."

"Well, clearly she's been occupied with other things. I mean, *clearly*."

I snatched the flier and held it up to my face. There was a lot to process here. To begin with, the whole point of this fieldtrip was to experience exciting and contemporary theater in the heart of New York City. The itinerary included lectures at NYU and Colombia and three Broadway plays, the most compelling of which was "this year's hot new musical," *The Fabulous Foibles of Fr. Fitzpatrick*, from debut playwright Charley Campbell. If this wasn't news enough, the picture on the flier showed that Charley was pregnant: seven or eight months at least.

"Jesus," said Stephen. "Think it's yours?"

"Good evening, everyone. Thank you for coming tonight."

The room suddenly fell silent as five hundred pairs of eyes narrowed on the thin, brown man standing at the podium. I couldn't have told you what former-Prince Ramesh Aggarwal looked like before he lost his bet to Weatherfield, but the man as presently composed resembled an old-school Catholic monk, one of those guys who used to illuminate manuscripts and chant Gregorianly while the rest of Europe was busy dying of the plague. Ramesh wore a shapeless grey robe with a rope belt. He had on dusty sandals and thick reading glasses. He appeared perfectly content onstage. Unnervingly content, actually. Only cult members ever look like that, and then the next thing you know, they're drinking Kool-Aid.

"Before we begin," he said, "I wanted to say a few words about my friend, William Weatherfield. As many of you know, William and I entered into a serious wager last spring, the results of which have led us here, to the deserts of Arizona, to hone our craft and grow deeper in our shared vocation. Strange as it sounds, poetry has made us both intensely happy, which I would not have predicted a year ago. In fact, at that time, I believed I would win our bet within a matter of weeks, if not days, but obviously this was far from the truth. I know now that I was mistaken in my assumptions. I considered William to be a man of excess and indulgence, someone with real appetite for the fat of life. What I didn't realize was that this appetite was borne of habit, not inclination, for William had never actually tasted of the higher pleasures he professed to worship. Sex, drugs, sloth: these were the things he knew. Art, spirituality, and transcendence all lay beyond."

While Ramesh continued his introduction, I reexamined the flier of Charley and her hit play. In the picture, she had her arms thrown around two other women, actresses most likely. Her great belly was round as a full moon, and her mouth was stretched open in laughter. Even with the choppy print, I could sense a strange energy emanating from the woman I loved. She was…what was it exactly? Oh, right. That's it. She was happy. Happier than I'd ever seen her.

"Passion," said Ramesh. "From the Latin, *pati*, meaning to suffer or endure. It wasn't until our wager that William truly entered into the life of an artist, forgoing all unnecessary comforts in the service of his calling. This was not an easy road. Long and treacherous, paved with fear, loneliness, and hours of drudgery: many who try this path will surely stumble along the way, but it is the road William and I have chosen, and it has led us here to you this night that you may enter into our suffering and share in our transcendence."

The audience burst into applause as Ramesh stepped aside, and a thin sandy-haired Englishman approached the stage. Weatherfield was indeed very handsome. He was dressed much like his disciple (only with white robes instead of grey), and his eyes were the striking blue color of the sea. To put it simply, he had the look of a prophet about him, and fittingly, his voice, though by no means thunderous, carried an undeniable weight, which silenced the crowd as soon as he began to speak.

"Good evening," he said. "I'm going to read you a love poem."

"Oh, Christ," I thought, scanning the room for Tobit. I spotted the kid on the far side of the atrium about halfway back from the stage. He was looking seriously pissed off at this point, which was strange, because I'd never seen him even a little bit angry.

"Where are you going?" whispered Stephen.

"I got to make sure he doesn't do something stupid."

"Wait. Hold on. I'll come with you."

Up at the podium, Weatherfield unfolded a single sheet of paper. He said that his poem was not like other love poems. He said that many of us would find it weird and unsettling, but he thought it was beautiful, and he wanted to share it.

"It's called 'The Archeologist,'" he said, and then began to read:

174

The old men were drinking scotch and talking dynasties
when we met. It was all so deathly
boring. They put their glasses to their dry lips and sucked
down the liquor. Their cheekbones hung like sickles under
their eyes.
Their skin was rough and brittle like old parchment.
Death snatched at their bones like an ivory hook.

But you were there among them,
the only strip of life I'd found
in that dry, dead land where even the trees were stone.
You had a headache and had to lie down,
and who could blame you
what with the talk and your brain
sitting in that jar across the room?

When the others had drowned themselves to sleep
and staggered off to their funeral sheets spun of worm guts,
we were finally alone. My fingers trembled around my
glass
as I looked into your obsidian eyes and then, like a coward,
at my shoes. You were so beautiful lying there, wrapped in
your bridal cloth,
and it was the beauty, not the scotch,
sparked that ancient fire in my blood,
and together we made sweet, forbidden

Small talk. I asked where you had studied only to let slip
I'd earned my doctorate at Oxford.
I could feel the warm blood beneath my cheeks
as words began spilling from my lips like grains of
nonsense sand.
It is always hard talking to a woman,
especially the beautiful ones,
the ones with paste of cloves and wild honey in their limbs

and cinnamon in their skulls.

I put down the scotch and took your hand
in my own. Your fingers were thin and delicate and
cold. But I could warm them. If I put them to my chest
where the empty space was,
where years and years of books had ripped the bleeding
muscle from my ribs
and stuffed a scarab wrapped in sheepskin in its place,
I could warm them. Why do people lie to one another?
Because lies are sweet and ancient and beautiful things.

"Tobit, stop!" I shouted as Weatherfield finished his poem,
but my words were drowned out by the thunder of applause.
"What's he doing?" said my brother.
"This is no good!" I said.
I took off running for the stage with Stephen hot on my
heels. We were too late, though, too far away. There was too
much ground to make up, and Tobit, surprisingly quick for a
person his size (maybe Coach Moses should've pegged him to
play linebacker instead of offensive tackle), was at the podium
before either of us could stop him. I'll never forget the look on
Weatherfield's face as he stared down my friend, at least twice
his size. It was an expression not of fear or even surprise.
There was only acceptance there—calm and considered—as if
he'd seen the punch coming all along.

32

The head of campus security—a tired-looking Latino sitting at his desk, sipping coffee from an Arizona Diamondback's commemorative thermos—told me again that this was, quote, "not like it is in the movies, *Padre*. You can make as many calls as you need. In fact, here, take my cell if you want, but remember, we're just waiting on Weatherfield to get back from Health Services. So long as he doesn't press charges, you're all free to go."

Kind words given the circumstances. Presently, however, I was too concerned with other matters to acknowledge them as such. I snatched the man's phone and punched in the first nine digits of Charley's number. Then I hesitated.

"Something the matter?"

"Mind if I have some privacy?"

"This is *my* office," said the officer.

I told him of course, and I was terribly sorry, but I really would like to, you know…it was a sensitive conversation.

"Fine," he said, and stood up with a sigh. I had ten minutes. After that, he was putting me back in the holding cell with the others.

"Thank you," I called after as the door slammed shut behind him. Once he was gone, I punched in the last number and then waited for the call to connect. It was intolerable purgatory those six to eight seconds. Finally the dial tone started buzzing. One ring. Two rings. Three rings. Four rings. I was just about to give up all hope when suddenly there came that glorious click followed immediately by Charley, breathless and anxious, saying, "Hello? Hello? This is Charley Campbell. Hello? I didn't miss you, did I?"

My first thought (stupidly optimistic) was that she'd been waiting for my call all day cooped up in a dark room somewhere with nothing but her phone to keep her company. This illusion was promptly dispelled, for no sooner did I answer, "Hello, Charley," than there followed a heavy silence, which was in turn followed by an even heavier, "*Leo?*"

"Yes, it's Leo. Who did you think it was?"

"What do you mean, who did I think it was? What number is this? Where are you? I'm waiting for a very important call, just so you know, so I can't talk long."

I asked her who she was expecting.

"It's not important."

"You just said it was."

"I mean it's not important for *you*," she corrected. "Oh, hell, it's *The New York Times*, okay? Now what do you want? Where are you?"

"Tucson," I told her. "Didn't you read my last email?" Just then, a dark thought popped into my head. "Have you read *any* of my emails? I've been writing nearly every day. Jesus, if all those letters went unread, I might as well—"

"Calm down. I read the emails," she said. "All eighty-six of them by last count. You should really hold onto them, maybe even send them off to a publisher. *The Collected Letters of Fr. Leopold Murphy*. Can you imagine how that would look on a coffee-table?"

I stood and began pacing around the campus security office. The room, poorly lit, was cluttered with paperwork and outdated computer monitors. A real-life fax machine occupied one corner. Opposite, there sat a table with half a birthday sheet cake. Yellow. Cream cheese icing.

"If you read the emails," I said, "then when were you going to answer them?"

Silence on the other end of the line.

"Charley? Hello?"

"I'm here, Leo. I heard you."

"Well?"

She took her sweet time answering, and when she finally did get around to it, all she gave me was some bullshit about being incredibly busy lately.

I called her on it, and she snapped, "Well, it's the truth. Not everyone's been on vacation for the past eight months. Some of us have real responsibilities to deal with. We can't just up and leave whenever we damn well feel like it."

"Right," I said, getting angry now, too. "Real responsibilities. I can imagine. In fact, I bet it's been a fucking whirlwind for you lately." I took the flyer out of my pocket and unfolded it on the table next to the sheet cake. Charley's pixilated image stared up at me in all its pregnant glory. I read to her, "Reserve your tickets for the hottest new musical of the season. From the talented pen of debut playwright Charley Campbell comes an ingenious romp of faith and infidelity. *The Fabulous Foibles of Fr. Fitzpatrick.* Be careful what you pray for."

I crumpled the flyer into a ball inside my fist. Charley had gone quiet again, so the only sound I heard was the buzz of a nearby computer.

After a few seconds: "Listen, Leo—"

"When were you going to tell me about the baby?" I cut her off.

Silence again. This time, it was a full minute before either one of us spoke.

"I'm waiting for an answer."

"What are you mad about?" she asked. "The play or the baby?"

"Both," I nearly shouted. "I mean neither. Jesus Christ, can't you tell I'm terribly happy for you?"

"You sure sound like it."

I collapsed into the security officer's chair and said, "You have to admit, this is a big thing to keep from someone."

"The play doesn't open for another week."

"I'm talking about our kid obviously."

"Oh."

"It is *our* kid, isn't it?"

"What?"

"Never mind."

"No, why would you ask me that? Why would you say, 'Is it *our* kid?'"

I gave a tug on my collar.

"You know Jerry couldn't…"

"Of course."

"Then why—"

"Look, I don't know, okay. I guess it's just been a long time since I've seen you. I wasn't sure…"

"You weren't sure what?" Charley said. "You weren't sure that I hadn't turned into a big slut since you've been gone?"

"Please don't put words in my mouth."

"I bet you were *hoping* this kid wasn't yours. Whew! What a relief that would've been. A huge weight off your shoulders."

"Charley, stop it. I'm ecstatic, alright? We made a child together. This is a wonderful development."

Silence again.

"Hello?"

"Don't think this changes things, Leo."

"What?"

"Between us. Just because you knocked me up, that doesn't means I'm going to run off with you and get married. I'm perfectly capable of raising this baby on my own. I've got tons of money because of the play, and New York is full of culture and good public schools, so don't think for a second that I'll need your help with anything."

These last words hit me like a punch to the gut. I sat there, slumped in the security officer's chair, feeling less like a flesh and blood person and more like a giant deflated balloon man.

"Won't you let me see him?" I asked.

Charley let out a deep sigh. "Her," she said. "And yes, of course you can see her. I'm not a monster. I won't keep you from our daughter."

Now she sounded deflated, too, and without the proper amount of air, neither of us could hope to keep the conversation going.

"I really do need to let you go, Leo. *The Times*. They'll be calling any minute. Please, I don't want to miss them."

"No, of course not."

"Goodbye," said Charley

"Goodbye," I said.

33

Back in the lock-up, I found Tobit sitting alone on a bench in the corner holding an icepack against the knuckles of his right hand. He was looking pretty sullen, as you can imagine, and wrapped up as he was in thoughts of betrayal and lost love, he didn't so much as turn his head when I entered.

Neither did Stephen for that matter.

My brother, likewise absorbed, occupied the opposite corner of the cell. Instead of sitting on the bench that was provided, he knelt upon the floor, bent over a collection of papers. There were three sheets in total, two of which were covered in a dark, spidery script, and the third, half blank, but filling up fast.

"While confined here in the Birmingham city jail, I came across your recent statement calling our present activities unwise and untimely."

Stephen glanced up but had no comment regarding my MLK impression. His ballpoint—momentarily frozen—hung approximately two centimeters above the page.

"Come on," I told him. "It's a bit early to crack up and start writing letters. We've only been in here a few hours. Where did you get those supplies anyway? I swear these jailers are too lenient. That pen would make a perfect shiv."

While my brother returned to his composition, I sat on the bench behind him and leaned back against the bars, which were uncomfortable, but the best I could manage under the circumstances. I was too damn tired to do much of anything except exist.

"Well, it's official," I said. "Charley's pregnant and the baby's mine."

A short pause from the scribe below.

"Did you hear that, Tobit? I'm a father now. I mean in the literal sense. I believe cigars and champagne are in order."

"Congratulations, Fr. Murphy."

"Jesus, don't sound too thrilled about it."

After a few last marks, Stephen set down his pen and pushed himself up from the floor. Then he sat next to me and put his arm around my shoulder, which was actually the most intimate embrace we'd shared in years.

"You don't smell too good," I told him.

"Are you scared, Leo?"

I nodded.

"Me, too," he said. He took his arm away and picked up the three sheets from the floor. He asked me to read them over if I didn't mind, and I told him, sure, what the hell else was I going to do in here?

The first letter was addressed to his wife:

Dear Kitty,

It's me, your husband. I'm safe and sound and so sorry about everything. You're a better person than I deserve, and the same goes for all three of our beautiful children. It was wrong to disappear on you. I guess I've been afraid recently and also confused about a lot of things. I know that doesn't excuse what I've put you through, but it's the truth. For a long time now, I've been selling happiness and certainty and peace-of-mind, and it's been gnawing at me from the inside, because I don't really have these things to offer. I've only been pretending that I do, but I can't pretend any more. I have to start living differently. I don't know what this means exactly, but what I do know is that I want you and the kids to be a part of my new life. Maybe this is an unfair request given everything I've done, and maybe you'll want nothing to do with me from now on, but I couldn't not ask, and I can't not hope.

The second letter was for Gertrude.

Dear Cold Hearted Bitch [or whatever he actually wrote],
    If you haven't thrown this into the trash, let me start by offering a long-overdue apology. It was wrong of me to treat you the way I did. I'm not saying we should've stayed together (good lord, I think we can both agree on that!), but just because we grew into two very different people, that didn't give me the right to act so cruelly. If I could, I'd take back 95% of the things I said to you in our last months as man and wife. No, I don't think you're a wicked person, and no, I don't think you're destined for an eternity of Hell-fire. I hope, given enough time, you can say the same about me, but even if you can't, I just wanted to tell you that I'm sorry. I mean for everything. You know all the ugly details, so there's no need for a full recap. Let me just say that there was a period of my life in which I loved you more than anything in the whole world. Even though those years are over now, I still care about you, and I still wish you well.

Finally, there was a letter for me.

Dear Leo,
    I wish we'd kept in better touch. This was probably as much my fault as it was yours. I know I've never been a very good brother. For most of my life, I actually kind of hated you. Can you blame me, though? You were so talented at

everything, and also very good-looking. And you were sometimes a jerk, too, like when you broke my collar-bone and stole Caroline McBride. But it doesn't matter. I forgive you for that and for everything else. I hope you can forgive me. I admit to taking a selfish pleasure in my DVD sales while you were struggling with your reassignment. It's sort of funny. After all this time, I still can't help feeling competitive. On the other hand, now that fate or God or luck or whatever has brought us together again, it occurs to me that you aren't quite the asshole I remember. Who's changed, do you think, you or me? Either way, I'm glad you're back in my life. It was getting lonely up on that mountain. I didn't know it then, but I missed you.

"Jesus, Stephen, you're going to make me cry."

I handed back the letters and told him they all checked out spelling and grammar-wise, though in my experience, he shouldn't expect much in way of response. My brother set the pages aside and gave me a big hug. It was a nice moment really. Maybe I did tear up a little bit. Then, before things had a chance to get too sentimental, the head of campus security entered the room and announced, "You've got a visitor here."

We all looked up, even broken-hearted Tobit, because it was Madonna Garfield who was standing before us. She was exactly as my friend had described her: pale, skinny, black nail polish, purple lipstick. She wore a leopard-print miniskirt and platform boots that very nearly doubled her natural height. Her jacket—if you could call it that—was a contrivance of leather and iron spikes and probably contained many secret pockets in which mace, brass knuckles, switch-blades, etc. were housed. I noticed that the head of campus security was casting a suspicious and continuous glance in her direction. No doubt he was just as surprised as anyone that Madonna stood on his side of the bars, while the gentleman in clerics remained incarcerated.

"How's the hand, TP?"

No answer from Tobit.

"I saw the punch. I was sitting just a few rows from the front. You really walloped him, you know. There was at least 1d8 worth of damage there. Maybe even a critical hit."

Still no reply. Tobit, the poor kid, wasn't even maintaining eye contact, but had his arms crossed over chest and was staring at a portion of floor just in front of Madonna's boots.

"Who are you supposed to be, his priest?"

"Huh?"

"You want to help me out here?"

"Listen," I told her, "when it comes to relationships, I'm the wrong person to consult."

She turned back to Tobit as she walked up to our cell. With two hands on the bars, she squeezed her face through as far as it would go and said, "Can't we talk? I came here to see you. I wanted to apologize."

"Why didn't you write me?" he said.

"Oh," said Madonna. "Right. Well, I guess that is a reasonable question." She slumped down and also sort of wobbled in place as if her legs could no longer support the weight of her body, and the only thing keeping her upright was the fact that her skull was wedged between the bars of the cell. "I don't know. It's complicated."

"I don't think it's too complicated," said Tobit. "All you had to do was reply to an email or answer one of my calls."

"Sure."

"In fact, I think that sounds pretty simple."

Madonna frowned and said nothing for a few moments. Then: "I was sad, alright?"

Tobit looked up at her.

"That's the truth, TP. I know it sounds stupid, but I'm being honest. When I got here in the fall, shit there were just so many people, way more than I ever knew back home. And then I started classes, and all those teachers that had told me they really liked my story, well it turns out they didn't really like my other stuff all that much. They said my writing was derivative and immature and shocking for the sake of being shocking, and I felt really stupid, you know, to have abandoned you back in Mount Sinai and come all this way, and for what? Just so people could look at me funny and make jokes behind my back? Just so they wouldn't care about me at all?"

"But I cared about you," said Tobit. "I never stopped caring. All you had to do was write."

Madonna shook her head. "You don't understand. I was ashamed."

"Why?"

"Because I felt like a failure."

"But you were just a college freshman."

"That doesn't mean I didn't feel like a failure."

Tobit stood up now and marched over to her. Face to face, the discrepancy in mass was staggering. "What did you see in him?" he demanded.

"Who? William? I don't know. You heard him read. He's very talented."

"Great. Well, I'm sorry I'm not so *talented.*"

"Stop it, TP. You know that isn't what I mean. It's just that William thought my writing was really good. He said it was true and original, and he even defended me in class when everyone else was attacking. I guess he made me feel special. Is that such a bad thing to want to feel?"

"You were special before."

"I didn't *feel* that way."

"You were special to me," said Tobit. "How could you not feel it?"

Madonna stepped away from the bars and clutched her jacket with both hands such that her arms formed an X across her chest. She stared at Tobit for some time without saying anything. I thought she might start crying, or that he might start crying. In either case, it was about to get a hell of a lot more awkward for the rest of us. In the end, though, no tears came. Madonna lowered her arms and approached the cell. She put her hand up to Tobit's face and touched his cheek.

"Sometimes I don't think you really loved me, TP."

"How can you say that? What about all the time we spent together? Remember all those really deep conversations we shared?"

"I remember we played a lot of *Dungeons and Dragons*. I remember we did magic and talked about things that were never really going to happen. We were kids."

"It was just a year ago."

"We didn't know what we were saying."

"I knew what I was saying. I believed every word of it."

"But it wasn't real."

"It was real to me," said Tobit.

"Yeah?" said Madonna. "And how did that turn out? Don't you get it, TP? I cheated on you. *Cheated*. You have to admit it was wrong to put so much faith in me."

He shook his head and told her no.

"Then you really are still just a kid. You haven't learned a thing."

"That isn't true. I've learned lots of things. I've learned that the world is a pretty sucky place, for starters. I've learned that it's way easier to pay attention to your life than the suffering of others. I've learned that God, wherever He is, has some serious explaining to do. I've learned that the people you love the most in this world will hurt you the most. And I've also learned that despite all that, I still have to love," said Tobit, "because if I don't love, then how can I reasonably expect anyone else to? So that's what I'm doing, okay? Regardless of everything that's happened, I'm standing here, choosing to love you, hoping that you choose to love me back."

A moment of silence followed these words. Then, the next thing I knew, Tobit and Madonna were kissing each other through the bars very aggressively, and Stephen was saying,

"Wait a minute. What's happening?" and I was saying, "I think they just made up," and he was scratching his head, probably trying to decide whether what we were witnessing was some authentic emotional magic or just a couple of horny teenagers being idiots.

"It's magic," I told him.

"Huh?"

"Just go with it."

"What are you talking about, Leo?"

"Knock it off, you two. No one likes that much PDA. For Christ sake's, there's an officer of the law present."

But the head of campus security—a real softy as it turns out—was just standing there, blowing his nose into a handkerchief, saying, "You're free to go. All of you. You're all free. Halleluiah!"

34

"Excuse me, sir, do you mind if I..."

"Oh, pardon me."

I looked up from my program as the young woman smiled and squeezed past me to her seat.

"I'm excited, too," she said.

"What?"

"I said I'm excited, too."

I gazed at her curiously, this girl, wiry and pale, with thick, dark-rimmed glasses and gangly limbs that didn't quite match her dress. My befuddlement must've been apparent, for she explained, "Your hands are shaking. Mine, too, figuratively speaking."

"Oh. Yes, so they are." I returned my attention to the program, specifically the cast list, where I was pleased to discover that the actor portraying Francis Fitzpatrick was at least rather handsome in a grizzled, roguish kind of way. Charley's character—she was called Helena in the play—wasn't too hard on the eyes either. Jerry was also there, except his name had been changed heavy-handedly to Goodman.

"Of all the folks in my playwriting workshop, I was the only one to score tickets."

"Lucky you."

"Charley Campbell is an inspiration," said the girl.

I nodded politely.

"I'm going to stick around after tonight's performance and get her autograph."

This was my plan, too: an ambush at the stage door. I'd been imagining the climactic scene all afternoon.

"What a beautiful theater! You know, I've probably walked by it a thousand times, but I've never actually been inside before. It's so...oh, sorry, the lights are dimming. I'll shut up now."

As the orchestra launched into the overture, I felt a clenching in my stomach like I was falling down a very deep hole with nothing soft to catch me at the bottom. This had little to do with the music itself, which was light and frolicking, and spoke more to the sense of impending doom which had been growing in me exponentially over the last hour. When the overture finished, a single spotlight appeared onstage, illuminating Helena sitting before an organ. She struck a key, and the pipes bellowed.

"From the top," she said.

A man lit up, singing, "The Heavens are telling the glory of God!"

"You're a little flat."

A woman now: "And all creation is shouting for joy!"

"I don't believe you, Minerva."

"Come dance in the forest, come play in the field," chimed in two additional choir members, equally off key.

Helena winced. "Jesus, save us."

Then altogether now, the stage flooded with light: "And sing, sing to the glory of our God!"

With "The Canticle of the Sun" continuing to limp along in the background, Charley Campbell (I mean Helena Whatever) leapt full force into the opening song, a bouncy, sharp-witted number entitled "Sing me to the G-Spot," that managed to conflate spiritual, sexual, and professional frustration into one glorious Freudian romp. Sample lyrics included: "Cure me of my leprosy. / Send me into ecstasy. / Holy God, I long for thee. / Don't deny me, let me scream!" The character of Goodman was introduced halfway through ("Got a damn vasectomy!"), and then came Fr. Fitzpatrick, an ex-missionary still hot from the jungles of Africa, who possessed a not insubstantial degree of sex appeal, which got Charley, I mean Helena, so wet in the panties that by the end of the song, Goodman was forgotten, the chorus dismissed, and Fr. Fitz had mounted, or rather was being mounted, atop the unwieldy pipe organ.

"Alleluia," screamed Helena at the appropriate moment.

I may or may not have given a silent fist pump.

The audience began to applaud, but then stopped as soon as poor Goodman wandered back onstage. He was humming the tune of "Sing me to the G-Spot" while mopping up the church floor. What followed was a bit of clever stunt design. The pipe organ, rocking via Helena and Fitz's vigorous hump-fest, was made to teeter on edge just as Goodman passed underneath it. One last thrust was all it took. Helena screamed (this time out of fear), the organ toppled, and just like that her husband was crushed. The whole thing happened so fast and with such verisimilitude (there must've been a trapdoor involved) that more than a few female audience members added their own panicked voices to the production. A final detail: all that remained of Goodman were his work boots, protruding from the organ like the ruby-slippered feet of the Wicked Witch.

"Oh my God, what have I done?" cried Helena.

"You mean, 'What have *we* done?' baby," corrected Fr. Fitzpatrick, who then slapped her on the ass and said, "Well, I guess I'm gonna have to say a funeral now."

The metamorphosis was as abrupt as it was extreme. One moment Fitzpatrick was a suave, sultry Casanova tangoing Helena across the church pews. The next thing I knew, he was an overgrown frat boy with a beer gut. In the following scene, Goodman's corpse was rolled onstage for the funeral, and Helena began singing a very tearful and guilt-ridden eulogy only to be interrupted at various intervals by Fitz's snide remarks. The number turned combative and then eventually climaxed with a screaming match over Goodman's body in which Helena (incensed to the point of sickness) projectile-vomited into her dead husband's casket.

"This holy man has turned my stomach," she sang alone onstage afterwards in a minor key.

I believe at this point the aspiring playwright began tearing up, though I didn't look over to confirm.

"That's not how it happened," I muttered.

"Shhh!"

"He was my best friend. I was heartbroken, too."

What came next was sort of a time lapse montage of Helena's illness set to some super suspenseful, quasi-racist African drums and monkey-howling and lion-roaring, the conceit being (and by the way, there were also some cool red lighting effects) that Helena had caught something third-world venereal from ex-missionary Fitz.

Then, in the hospital:

"Well, lay it on me, Doc."

"It isn't Eeeeeeboooolaaaaaa!"

"Okay, that's good."

"No chance of malaaaaaaiiiiiiiiiiriaaaaaa!"

"Whew, dodged a bullet."

"So long to Chooooooolerrraaaaaa!"

A chorus of nurses joined them onstage, everybody wearing puke green scrubs and singing a catchy tune that dispelled Helena's fears of Syphilis, Gonorrhea, HIV/AIDS, and Chlamydia in that order.

"But then what is it? Why am I sick? / If not a virus I caught from his prick?"

The lighting and music turned very serious.

"Honey, sit down. We've got bad news to tell ya. / This Father Fitzpatrick, he ain't a good fella. / The bug that he gave

193

you, it's the worst STD. / I'm sorry, Miss Charley. It's pregnancy."

A disappointed trombone accompanied the final mismetered line. Then the music picked up again with Helena ("Hysterical Helena" the Doc now called her) vocalizing panic at breakneck tempo. I found myself tapping my foot while the option of abortion was brought up, then tabled, then brought up again, then finally dismissed with, "I'm a good Catholic girl who loves church songs and Jesus. / Get back, all you doctors. Stay away from my fetus." (Technically it was still an embryo at this point.) The song ended with Helena marching back to the church and telling Fr. Fitzpatrick the news, which hit the guy pretty hard, you can imagine.

"What now, God?" he sang to the rafters.

"What now, God?" Helena joined in.

There followed a haunting duet entitled "The Lovers' Complaint," in which the two main players took a good hard look at their lives, or rather the lives they'd lived and wished to live. We learned, for example, that Helena, just like her author, was an unhappy choir director and longed instead for the bright lights of Broadway.

"I could've starred in Kiss Me Kate. / Instead I'll kiss my little girl, / And all my dreams goodbye." (Barf.)

Fitz, meanwhile, lamented giving up his missionary work: "I became a priest to change hearts, not diapers." (Double barf.)

By the end, the couple was united not so much by any feelings of affection but rather a mutual servitude embodied in Helena's ever-rounding belly. This was (unsurprisingly) not enough to keep them together. As soon as Helena was offstage, Fitz began confessing how he couldn't bear to live a domesticated life. The only option he saw was to steal Goodman's life insurance claim and then continue his adventures, which was a very unfair portrayal, in my opinion, seeing as I'd specifically asked Charley to run away with me, and anyway, I didn't even know she was pregnant at that point.

"Isn't this great?" whispered the aspiring playwright.

"Sure."

"Charley Campbell is a fucking rock star."

Time jumped forward again, and in the following scene, Helena was standing over a crib, alone, cooing to a baby girl, when a sound at the door announced the mailman.

"A letter from Daddy! How exciting? Where could he be?"

Helena tore open the envelope and began to sing the contents as a sort of lullaby. It turned out that Fr. Fitzpatrick was back in Africa. He'd resumed his missionary work and had many fascinating exploits to report.

"Yesterday I converted a pygmy! / Tomorrow, I set sail for Sidney!"

After a few bars of Helena singing, Fr. Fitzpatrick joined in and then took over the song altogether, the effect being that now he was the one narrating the letter. He'd returned to his dashing ways, sweaty and handsome, clerics ripped apart by lions' claws, revealing a chest of chiseled muscle. While widow and child remained rooted to the bedroom-setting upstage right, the rest of the stage was now dominated by a massive frigate cutting through the ocean.

"Oh, no!" cried Helena, clutching the letter. "Listen to what comes next."

It was an eighteenth century pirate ship complete with cannons and black sails and a long, shaky plank. A series of tremendous reports echoed through the theater. The smell of gunpowder wafted over us. The pirates, looking more Penzancian than Somalian, swung aboard the frigate and began attacking the crew with plenty of swashbuckling, pistols misfiring, etc. More than one person was thrown spectacularly overboard, falling at least thirty feet before crashing into a pool of water set up just in front of the stage.

"This thing must've cost a shitload to produce," I said.

"Avast, ye mateys!" shouted the leader of the pirates, Captain Shaggybeard, according to the program. "Look there. That holy man fights with the strength of ten elephants!"

Indeed, Fr. Fitzpatrick seemed to be the only passenger competent in hand-to-hand combat.

"Capture him, lads! We could use a chaplain with some spunk!"

A wonderful fight ensued, which the orchestra soundtracked with funny-sounding woodwinds and crashing brass. It ended with Fr. Fitz tied up and given a choice between a) walking the plank, or b) joining this motley crew.

"I decided to become a pirate," he narrated to Helena, "not out of fear of death, but with a deep conviction in the grace and power of God, that He may, through His love, touch the blackest hearts and make them pure again."

Fr. Fitz's faith was then tested over the course of the following scenes, while Helena (they were still maintaining the whole epistolary conceit) would sometimes interrupt the action, either adding her own wry commentary or editing out sections she deemed inappropriate for children. No need to document every detail of the production. Let's just say there was plenty of looting and whoring to go around. Eventually, though, Fr. Fitz got through to the miscreants during a climactic storm scene in which Captain Shaggybeard, realizing that his ship was just one big wave away from Davy Jones' Locker, made a deal with the priest that if he delivered them from the tempest then the entire crew would convert to Christianity. Naturally, God stepped in and calmed the waters in no time. After this, the pirates gave up their barbarous ways and became agents of good, sailing the seven seas, feeding the hungry, giving drink to the thirsty, clothing the naked, etc.

But all this was beside the point.

And I mean that literally as well as figuratively.

When she'd started reading the letters, Helena and baby were restricted to a modest portion of the stage very far away from the audience, but as the musical progressed, the staging began to shift with Fr. Fitz and the pirates squeezed into a smaller and smaller corner until at last it was almost comical to watch twenty plus men and an enormous schooner crammed into a space no wider than a dining room table.

The plot, too, had shifted focus. Yes, Fr. Fitz's letters were still being read, but his adventures were reported more and more concisely, like the cliff notes version of the story instead of the real thing. And between the letters, a relationship was forming between Helena and her child, a precocious girl ominously named Elektra (everyone called her "El" for short) who developed from cooing infant to rebellious teen over the course of about forty minutes.

And it was really her play now. El's, I mean. We watched her grow. We watched her mature. She would listen to her father's letters first with fascination, then with some quiet doubt, finally with downright, almost militant skepticism.

"How did he wrestle Bengal tigers in China? Bengal is in India."

"I don't know, honey. Maybe they escaped from a zoo."

"And piranhas are a freshwater fish. You don't find them in the ocean."

At last, El had had enough of these dubious epistles. Just when Fitz and his saintly pirates were about to foil an intricate assassination plot on the Holy See, El's new boyfriend Chip pulled up on a Harley and sang, "Let's ditch this place, El Dorado."

Hither came the girl in red lipstick and black leather jacket, fishnet stockings, the whole nine yards, pausing just long enough to call back to her mother, "Sorry, but I gotta dust. You don't see Daddy the way he is. Maybe someday you will."

There was one last heartbreaking number before intermission, Helena's "Write Me." Then the curtains fell, and the lights went up.

35

"Hold on," I said. "Run that by me again."

"Which part?" said the aspiring playwright. She sucked her Marlboro down to a flaming nub, which she used to light another cigarette before crushing the first under her heel. Then she let out the smoke and said, "You want another one?"

"Please."

She tossed me the pack, which I almost dropped, I was so jittery.

"Thanks."

"Uh-huh."

"The part about male hegemonic imperial undertones."

"Oh, sure, it's not that complicated."

We stepped aside to make room for more smokers out on the street. Everybody was buzzing about the play. There were about fifty different conversations going on at once.

"Basically you have to think about the piece operating on all these different levels simultaneously. Like obviously there's the feminist perspective, but there's also this whole post-colonial tilt that's like super fucking interesting in its own right."

"Okay, but what—"

"And don't even get me started on religion. No offense, but even you have to admit the Catholic Church can be repressive."

I had no qualms admitting this. In fact, I confessed that within the past year, I myself had been deemed a heretic.

"No shit," said the girl, breathing out smoke through her nostrils. "Heretic. I didn't know they still kicked that term around. What did you do, pass out free condoms and tell people it was okay to screw?"

"Well, no, not exactly."

"Listen, I'd love to pick your brain sometime. I'm working on this thing right now. I don't know what it is just yet, maybe a one-act, maybe a full play. Regardless, the main character...I guess there are two main characters...one's this Jewish girl from like a super orthodox family, and then there's this Catholic guy—" She took a long drag from her Marlboro and said, "God I love cigarettes. I think if I had unlimited cigarettes and coffee I could probably write a fucking folio of genius shit."

"Yeah," I said, not wanting to kill her buzz.

Suddenly a look of intense sadness passed across her face. "I don't mean that. I'm just talking out my ass."

"Um..."

"I think I'm depressed, Father."

"Oh no."

"I mean it. Maybe not clinically, like I don't need electroshock therapy or anything like that, but I'm sad, you know, deeply. It feels like the way life is just isn't suited for me. Or maybe I'm the one not suited for the way life is. God, what a bullshit way to say that. Anyhow, I keep writing and writing and writing, and it's like a compulsion, only the compulsion makes no sense, because my shit isn't any good and it's not like I particularly enjoy it, the writing I mean. It's just...Christ, how do I explain it? It's like I have this belief—and belief is the right word, because it's definitely not rational, it's definitely some genre of faith—that if I can just write a fucking killer play then it will all be worth it, you know? I want to create something beyond myself. Something good and meaningful. But I just can't do it. You understand?"

She looked up at me through the smoke. It was beginning to rain again, and a lot of the other smokers were tossing aside their cigarettes and heading back inside the theater. I told her it was funny, but I was having a serious case of déjà vu.

"No shit?"

"You sound a lot like Charley Campbell."

She smiled, then laughed to herself and rolled her eyes. "Man, don't compare me to her. I mean, I appreciate it, but you gotta understand, I'm not Charley Campbell. I don't have the story she does. It would be wrong of me to pretend I do."

I started to argue this point, but she cut me off.

"Seriously, Father, I know what I'm talking about. At this point, everything that I'm writing, it's just adding to the noise. Didn't you notice Fitzpatrick and the pirates, how at first they were dominating the stage, but then gradually, they got squeezed off into one tiny corner?"

"What are you saying?"

She sucked on her cigarette. "It's a metaphor, you know. Sometimes they need absence. Certain people at least. Otherwise they get choked and can't grow. We hear over and over again to find our voice and tell our story, but maybe the noble thing isn't always to tell your story. Maybe sometimes it's better to just shut up and let someone else tell hers. Anyway, that's why I'm considering early retirement from this whole playwriting charade I've been perpetuating since adolescence. My parents will be thrilled, I'm sure. Mom's probably got a whole list of contacts for me to call." The girl finished her last Marlboro and let it slip through her fingers and onto the sidewalk. She didn't step on it, though, like she had the others. She let it burn itself out. "I'm getting wet. You think we should head back in?" She looked at me. "Father?"

"Sorry. I was thinking about something else."

"That's cool. I was just spilling my existential guts over here."

I told her not to worry. I'd been listening the whole time, even more intently than she could imagine. "You think I could have one more cigarette?"

"They don't let you smoke inside."

"It's for the road."

36

When I look back now at the two and a half months I stayed with my brother and his wife, Kitty, I think to myself, what a peculiar house guest I must've appeared to their children. Here I was, this forty-eight year old stranger, crazy Uncle Leo, arriving one day completely out of the blue with nothing in terms of luggage save the clothes on my back. Mary, the littlest one, must've thought I'd caught something contagious in San Juandigo because whenever I entered a room, she would immediately freeze and cover her mouth.

"Stop that, you silly bee," Kitty often scolded from the kitchen.

But Mary was right to be cautious. I imagine I looked in those first days if not disease-ridden then at the very least disease-probable. My beard, normally quite trim, had become a bushy, ulotrichous mess, and my skin had turned so dark and leathery from the Caribbean sun that one day I overheard the two older children, Peter and Paul, arguing about whether I was an Indian of the Subcontinent or of North America.

The kids were drawn to me, I think, because I was mysterious and possibly dangerous. Often I heard them sneaking around the hall just outside my bedroom where they would press their ears to the door or else employ a pint glass so as to amplify the sound. I assume my mad ramblings only stoked their curiosity. For the first few weeks after my arrival, I was perhaps less than one-hundred percent altogether in the mental stability department. Many hours I spent alone, rereading the emails I'd written to Charley. I hardly ate or spoke to anyone.

"Call her again," Kitty suggested one night at the table over leftover cake wedges and decaffeinated coffee. "You two have a baby together. You need to talk things out."

I told her that wasn't a good idea.

"Why?"

Well, there were many reasons. Charley was a hotshot playwright now and didn't need me bothering her. We'd left things on a sour note. I'd stolen a not-insubstantial sum of money and had no way of repaying it. Our affair may or may not have caused her late husband's death via some complicated understanding of karma.

"Honestly, though, the biggest reason I'm hesitant to reach out again…"

"Yes, Leo?"

"I think she just needs to be left alone a while longer."

Kitty wasn't satisfied by this conclusion, but she was a gentle woman and did not press the issue. Neither did Stephen, for that matter. My brother was teaching a biology course at the local community college for the summer, so he was gone most mornings and afternoons, but evenings we often spent together at the dinner table where he told me all about returning home: how he'd confessed his doubts and fears to Kitty, how he'd begged her forgiveness for abandoning the family, and how Kitty, as was her nature, welcomed him back with open arms.

It was better than he deserved, Stephen admitted, and I told him, "Good. If we all got what we deserved, then where would that leave us?"

It was nothing short of miraculous that we grew to become such dear friends during this period. It made me sad to think how we'd wasted half our lives as adversaries, especially when we shared so much in common deep down. As if to make up for all that lost time, our talks often stretched long into the night, especially on weekends when my brother would make a pot of real coffee, gleefully announcing that he need not arise early the following morning to teach class. The topics of our conversations were varied and many. We spoke of the past, of Mom and Dad, of Caroline McBride, of our adventures at St. Ignatius, of my time in the Seminary and his years in college. We spoke of Gertrude and Kitty and Charley and what love really is anyway.

But despite these joys, my stay wasn't always so blessed. There were points of boredom and apathy, even sadness approaching that which had sent me sailing in the first place.

"I'm starting to worry about you, Leo," said Kitty one day when I did not rise from bed until early in the afternoon. "You know you're welcome to stay with us as long as you need, but is this the best place for you to be?"

Most definitely it was not. Though my brother's home had been a welcome, even necessary respite upon my return from New York, it soon became clear that a man with no job in a comfortable suburban house was as good as dead. Many days I wasted away on the luxurious leather couch of the ironically termed "living" room, flipping through the magical box of light and sound. I watched a copious amount of trash to be honest. There was a program about the buying and selling of abandoned storage facilities to which I became particularly attached. I was highly invested in all the debates raging in the universe of sporting news, and on a network of old game shows, I watched people who were dead now win money.

Occasionally, mercifully, the children would join me on the couch. As my stay lengthened from days to weeks, they grew accustomed to my presence and even became quite bold around me. Mary would pilfer the remote when I wasn't looking and immediately switch the channel to some kids' show. She had an encyclopedic knowledge when it came to the TV. Though multiplication tables were beyond her, she could recite from memory the schedules of over a hundred programs at least. Her brothers, meanwhile, peppered me with questions during the commercials.

"Uncle Leo, why are you living with us?"

"Uncle Leo, do you have a girlfriend?"

"Uncle Leo, do you have a job?"

"Uncle Leo, are you a freeloader?"

"Uncle Leo, our dad said you were a priest once, but now you aren't?"

"Uncle Leo, what happened to you?"

Don't misunderstand. I don't mean to imply that my nephews subjected me to an inquisition. Or rather, what I really mean is that I welcomed the inquisition. I found their brashness refreshing. No tiptoeing around the delicate stuff. Get right to the heart of the matter.

"Why am I living with you? Because I have no house of my own and no money to afford one. Yes, I am most definitely a freeloader. I do not have a girlfriend per se, but there is a woman whom I love and with whom I have a child, and I still hold out hope that maybe one day, when she is ready, when I am ready, she will become my wife. I am no longer a priest because of an essay."

"Ugh, I hate essays," said Mary, without looking up from *iCarly* or whoever.

"Shut up," said Paul. "You only do book reports. Me and Peter do essays."

Peter, the oldest and most mature of the brood, encouraged by my frankness, pressed further, asking all sorts of questions involving sex and drugs.

"Why don't you talk to your parents about these things?" I said to him, exhausted.

"Because then I'd just have to go read Bible passages, and anyway, they don't know like you do."

Well, the kid had a point.

"I like it when we talk," said Mary, quite sweetly, "but can you please, please, *please* be quiet when the show comes back on?"

Aside from these daily lessons, the other thing that kept me sane was my correspondence via email with Tobit Portnoy.

Dear Fr. Murphy,

How are things with you? Madonna sends her regards. We have returned to Mount Sanai for the summer and are currently sharing an apartment in the seedy part of town. The cockroaches are not too big and politely scurry under the refrigerator when you turn on the light. Also, it is very exciting to see our neighbors featured on the nightly news. Sometimes I feel like I am living amongst celebrities. We have made friends with many African Americans. If you're wondering, I did attempt to reconcile with my family. Everyone was surprised to see me and even more surprised to hear my story. I believe I've won the respect of Amos and Eli, and my mother was moved to tears. My father, however, remains as hardhearted as ever. He refused to shake my hand, which was disappointing but expected, and he has not forgiven Madonna. I might've said some words to him which I regret now.

Dear Tobit,

Do not beat yourself up about your dad. From all reports, Sherwood is a difficult person to love. That is all I will say on the matter, for the man is still your father despite his shortcomings, and I would not expect a son of your high caliber to tolerate further unkind words (albeit true and well-intentioned). One more thing I will say on the matter: do not give up on him. Reconciliation may come eventually. As the famous Jesuit priest and geologist Teilhard de Chardin once wrote, we must "above all, trust in the slow work of God. We are quite naturally impatient in everything to reach the end without delay. We should like to skip the intermediate stages. We are impatient of being on the way to something unknown, something new. And yet it is the law of all progress that it is made by passing though some stages of instability—and that it may take a very long time."

Dear Fr. Murphy,

I like what that Chardin guy had to say. I think I will send that quote to my father along with a note of apology. On second thought, perhaps I will just send the apology. Sherwood doesn't have much respect for Frenchmen or Catholics. He's indifferent regarding geologists. Have you thought about how "the slow work of God" might relate to your relationship with Ms. Campbell? I've heard her play is quite good, though it makes me sad that you two aren't together, especially considering the baby. Madonna sends her regards again. Speaking of which, there's a point I'd like to make concerning my last email. There's no need to be concerned with our present housing arrangement. Though we are sharing a roof and a bedroom, we are not, as they say, living in sin.

Dear Tobit,

I am disappointed to learn that you are not living in sin. How long can a person survive without intercourse? I believe food is forty days, water a week. I shall consult the medical journals. To answer your question about Charley, don't go patting yourself on the back with any delusions of insight. Of course I have given it thought. Why else would I bring it up in the first place? You know I am helplessly self-absorbed. Anyway, speaking of "slow work," or more accurately, "no work," what am I to do with the rest of my life? I can't go on watching television forever. How are you getting along professionally? Have you returned to school? How do you afford that charming apartment of yours? One last inquiry: I'm currently imagining you and Madonna sleeping together in the same bed but with a massive broadsword stabbed through the mattress, thus partitioning sides and preventing hanky panky. I find this portrait very old-fashioned romantic and agreeable. If it is accurate, please confirm. If not, write nothing, and let me have my little joy.

Dear Fr. Murphy,

Madonna gets the bed. I sleep on an air mattress that deflates every night. Sorry to disappoint. Professionally, we are also struggling. Madonna was able to return to her old job at the Alamo Steakhouse, so she's the one literally bringing home the bacon these days. The work doesn't satisfy her, though. I, too, am restless. I tried reenrolling at Mount Sanai Southern Baptist High School, but the other students (and frankly some of the teachers) are so narrow-minded and immature that education is impossible. Currently, I'm studying for the GED, which I'll need if I'm to apply to the University of Arizona come fall. All the test-prep books I check out from the library are insultingly basic and a bit depressing because of it. Today, I was reminded that Ben Franklin invented electricity by flying a kite. This is a dubious claim, in my opinion, so I wrote in the margin that "God invented electricity. B. F. illuminated certain relevant properties, which is not the same thing, but also commendable." I'm confident the next person to brave these prep materials will be thankful for the clarification.

Dear Tobit,

I'm glad to hear you're pursuing your education despite the obstacles described. Take it from a deadbeat like me, there's nothing like hard work and a tangible goal to keep sadness away. Meanwhile, I'm forty-eight years old, unemployed, and mooching off my brother's DVD royalties. At this point, I could use a swift kick in the ass and a "get a job, ya bum." Instead, there are only soft words in this house. Random question: do you think Homer ever wrote a sequel to *The*

Odyssey? I like to imagine the wily Greek bickering with his wife in Ithaca. "Why have you grown so fat?" says Penelope. "When I left you twenty years ago, you weren't such a bitch," replies Odysseus. I admit there isn't much of a story there, but for obvious reasons, I've recently been kicking around the idea of disappointed homecomings. One bright note: the kids are a romp. Peter, Paul, and Mary ask very pointed questions, all three of them. Sometimes lately our conversations have even turned vaguely theological. It's nice to know I'm doing my part in training three little heretics. God knows their parents can't be trusted with such matters, bless their hearts.

We exchanged many emails like this. Often, composing these messages and reading Tobit's replies were the highlights of my day. I would stay up really late at night, taking the computer with me into the closet where I would sit next to boxes of floppy discs and old video games. It felt strange and exciting to be the only person awake in such a large house. The place was full of noises. Every time I heard the walls creak or the dishwasher kick on, I'd jump and snap my head and look around madly like I was hoarding porno magazines.

Then one night, there was a knock at the door.

"Hello, Leo? Are you still up?" Kitty entered, bearing two wedges of pound cake with strawberries and vanilla ice cream. She was confused at first to find my room lighted but empty, but then I moved the closet door open with my foot, and our eyes met, and she smiled. "There you are," she said softly, setting one of the dessert bowls down on the desk. The other she kept for herself. "Mind if I sit?"

"Of course. It's your house."

She cleared a space for herself on the bed, which was unmade. "What are you doing in there? Hiding?"

"Something like that."

I watched her take a bite that was equal parts cake, cream, and berry. The correctness of the proportions pleased me. I also enjoyed the nice clink of spoon on bowl.

"Why don't you come out and have some dessert?"

I told her thanks, but no.

"It's very yummy."

No doubt it was.

Kitty stuck her spoon into the cake and said, "Fine. If you're not going to come out here and get it, then I'm going to bring it in there for you."

Before I could stop her, she picked up the second bowl and advanced into the closet. Her hips were nearly the exact width of the doorframe, so there was nowhere for me to go except backwards. I hit up against the wall. There were stacks of dusty boxes all around me.

"Cozy in here, isn't it?"

Kitty handed me my bowl and then lowered herself slowly to the floor. We were facing each other, both sitting Indian style, with only maybe four inches between us. I didn't know what else to do, so I took a bite of cake.

"Don't tell the kids."

"Pardon?"

"About the dessert. You know they aren't allowed to have sweets after eight o'clock."

"Oh, right."

"They really like you, you know."

I shrugged.

"Seriously. They talk about you all the time. I'm so glad you've been able to stay with us these past few months and really get to know them."

I continued to eat, hoping that once all the cake and ice cream was gone, Kitty might leave, too. It's not that I didn't like the woman, but she was in my personal space, breathing my air, sitting in my closet. Never mind these things actually belonged to her and Stephen.

"Leo, I—" She hesitated when she saw me staring.

I looked down again, ashamed. An uncomfortable silence had fallen between us that not even pound cake could bridge. I wondered why she had come tonight.

"Leo, I wanted to thank you," she said at last. "For what you did for Stephen. Bringing him home. I've never thanked you properly, and I don't know what I would've done had he never come back from that island. You saved me, you know. You saved all of us. Our whole family."

I told her she was welcome, but to leave the kids out of it. If anything, I'd ruined her children what with my heretical lessons.

"I wouldn't say they were ruined, Leo."

"Maybe not ruined. Maybe just corrupted."

"Enlightened."

I shook my head. "The last time I tried enlightening anyone, I was called before the archbishop, and my life fell apart."

"I think children are more receptive to your wisdom than a bunch of dusty old priests," said Kitty.

"Careful what you say about dusty old priests. I'm basically one myself."

She smiled at me and set aside her bowl. "Have you given any thought to what you want to do now?"

I asked if she and my brother were finally kicking me out.

"No, but I think you should teach, Leo. I mean really teach, you know, like in a classroom with chairs and a chalkboard. You have a way with children, and besides, Stephen loves his classes at the community college. It gives him a sense of satisfaction to be helping people like that. It's a type of service, really."

I took a minute to think about this, eating the rest of my cake and ice cream, the latter of which had melted, making the former soggy and delicious. The strawberries offered a tart balance. It was true that before I'd left Chippewa County, I'd asked Charley to run away with me to New York where she could write her plays and I could teach theology. She'd laughed at the idea back then, but now here she was, a famous playwright, so how ridiculous could it be?

"Leo?"

"Honestly, I've never given it much thought," I admitted. "Teaching seems like such an authoritarian undertaking, and I've made it a habit all my life to resist authority. Would it be hypocritical to change course now? It reminds me of how all the juvenile delinquents you know as a kid grow up to become cops. More to the point, could I even get a job if I wanted one? Who would hire me? Are there really any principals out there desperate enough?"

Kitty just kept on smiling.

"What is it?" I asked her.

"Nothing. I'm imagining you in the classroom. What I would give to be a fly on that wall."

37

Tanner Baxter, whom I hated, had this certain way of sitting at his desk. First, he would throw down his books next to an open seat in the back row. Then he would undo the buttons of his sports coat and loosen the knot on his red-checkered tie. Then he would plant himself upon the chair, reclining to such an extreme obtuse angle (legs spread eagle, displaying maximum crotch) that one couldn't help but think of gangsta rappers low-riding around Compton, which was ridiculous since Baxter's parents were both lawyers pulling in six figures and Baxter played lacrosse, possibly the whitest and douchiest sport offered at St. Francis Xavier High School. He was varsity co-captain and annoyingly good at shoving others aside and putting the ball in the net. Rumor had it, he'd played football his Freshman and Sophomore years but then switched to lacrosse because he wasn't getting any playing time. This did not surprise me, as all the real athletes at Francis Xavier (read: black kids) either played football or basketball and usually both, while everyone else excelled at lacrosse, racquetball, water polo, fencing, sailing, equestrian, competitive trust fund investing, etc.

"Mr. Baxter, do you have something to add?"

"Huh?"

"Perhaps regarding the current topic of conversation?"

"My hand wasn't up, was it?"

The rest of the class tensed, wondering if I would JUG him. This was the Catholic equivalent of a detention: Justice Under God, or something to that effect. "Justice," by the way, usually consisted of an hour performing mindless arithmetic or declining Latin verbs. Sometimes janitorial work.

"No, Mr. Baxter," I said, "your hand wasn't raised, but I couldn't help overhearing your comments to Mr. Prescott." (Cole Prescott, that slimy, weasel-nosed waste of carbon!) "Now perhaps you'd like to share your insights with everyone else?"

Tanner Baxter looked around, taking stock of the situation. The clock on the wall read 8:40, which meant that there were ten minutes left in first period. He knew it wasn't wise to piss off a teacher so early in the morning, especially when that teacher hadn't had his coffee yet. Still, Mr. Murphy hardly ever gave JUGs. The requisite paperwork deterred him.

"Call on somebody else."

"Excuse me?"

"I don't know the answer. Call on somebody else."

Cole Prescott, whom I despised sometimes equally, sometimes even more than his fellow conspirator, gave a smirk that would've driven a lesser man to expletives.

"Vinnie has something to say," said Max Honnold, a kind-hearted boy who genuinely wanted to learn, and thus always strove for classroom harmony.

"Thank you, Mr. Honnold, but Mr. Stefano's comment can wait. I'm St. Lawrencing Mr. Baxter at present. I'll let you know when the grates have cooled."

Tanner Baxter scratched his groin through his khaki slacks. "Well?"

"Why was Jesus crucified?" he said lamely.

"Yes, good, I'm glad you can read the chalkboard. Now that—"

"He wasn't a Roman citizen."

214

The class stirred. There were some grins. Whispered comments were exchanged. Tanner Baxter, instead of getting embarrassed like any decent person would, instead reclined even farther into his desk and produced a very smug look like he'd just solved an impossible mathematics proof.

"That doesn't have anything to do with the Paschal Mystery," said Vincent Stefano, not quite out loud, but also not quite to himself.

"What's that?" said Baxter.

Stefano stiffened but said nothing. He kept his eyes down on his Bible and his notes.

"That's what I thought."

Vincent Stefano had a black eye today, which bothered me because he was unambiguously my favorite student. A thin, sandy-haired boy with a gentle gaze and a very deep way of thinking, Vinnie floated through the halls of Francis Xavier, not so much an outcast as an oddball. By that I mean he read novels for pleasure, didn't play sports, asked pertinent questions, and could hold a meaningful conversation with an adult. He cared about his education in a manner most others didn't. I hoped his black eye wasn't from some messy family abuse situation. I didn't think it was (his parents were quiet, thoughtful people much like him), but I also didn't think Vinnie was the sort of kid who regularly got into fistfights.

"Mr. Baxter, the question was theological, not historical."

"Huh?"

I glared at him.

Max Honnold whispered from a couple desks away, "We're talking about the Passion, man. Why did Jesus need to suffer?"

Tanner Baxter intertwined his sausage-thick fingers and cracked them one after another very loudly. He reminded me of an ape sometimes with his hairy knuckles and overdeveloped pecs.

"Course he needed to suffer. Had to die for our sins, didn't he?"

"Well said, Mr. Baxter. And aren't we glad he did? Anyone else?"

I called on Vincent Stefano even though he no longer had his hand raised. A look of mild surprise passed over the boy's face. He hesitated a moment, looking without looking at Tanner Baxter before commenting, "I think we need to draw a distinction between pain and suffering."

"Yes. Go on."

"Many people use them interchangeably, but the way I see it, they're two completely different things. Pain is like...well, it has an obvious purpose. Like the hot stove, you know? You feel the pain of burning so you don't leave your hand there and seriously damage it."

I nodded appreciatively.

"But suffering is different. Suffering is...harder to understand. There doesn't seem to be a point to it. Like depression, for example. What's the point of depression? I don't see one."

Max Honnold put his hand up. "Couldn't you say that the point of depression is to show that the depressed person needs to change his life in some way? Like if you're depressed because you have a bad job or an unhappy marriage."

Vincent thought a moment, but then shook his head. "I don't think that's the same thing. I don't mean sadness or frustration. I mean real depression. The kind you have to take medicine for. It's a very dark thing. Much darker than a bad job, even a bad marriage."

"If that's what you mean," said Max Honnold, "then you could pick a lot of things. Like what's the purpose of Alzheimer's or Parkinson's?"

"Or leukemia," I said, "leprosy, Lou Gehrig's disease."

They looked at me.

"Sorry. Pay no attention to crazy Mr. Murphy."

Vincent Stefano glanced at his notebook, flipping through a couple of pages before he found the one he was looking for. "I have a question, Mr. Murphy."

"Shoot."

"We were talking last week about whether or not God is even capable of suffering..."

"Yes, does everyone remember what Vincent is referring to?"

Max put his hand up. "Some theologians consider suffering a form of change. God cannot change. Therefore God cannot suffer."

"Therefore God cannot suffer," echoed vermin-countenanced Cole Prescott from the back row. Three times already this quarter I'd JUGed him for mimicking classmates. He had such a hard on for impressing Tanner Baxter, he just kept doing it.

I said quite loudly, "Mr. Prescott, if I were your father, I'd feel a certain obligation to discipline you, but since, thankfully, I am merely your theology teacher, and underpaid, I will pass the buck, so to speak, and instead tolerate your asshole nature for the remaining seven minutes of the period."

The class got very quiet, as it always did when I resorted to profanity.

"Thank you," I said to no one in particular. "Vincent, you were asking about suffering?"

The boy nodded, eager, determined. "What I wanted to know...well, let's say those theologians are right, and that God can't suffer. But what does that mean in regards to Jesus? I guess what I'm asking is, does the dual nature of Christ mean that he was capable of *human* suffering?"

A fair question. I let it sit a few moments, marinating. I'd say about half the class was checked out at this point, but at least ten or fifteen boys were still interested, which wasn't too bad first period so late in the semester.

"I think he was," said Max Honnold. "I mean, just look at him."

He pointed to the crucifix hanging over the chalkboard. Every room in Francis Xavier had one. It was one of the three staples of the school, along with American flags and boxy old television sets that used to run announcements but now just showed the time.

"Remember what they said in the video. A symphony of pain."

That's right. That's what they'd said. Specifically, the slogan belonged to Dr. Patricia O'Neil, who was either a doctor of medicine or theology, it was impossible to tell. She spoke with equal authority on both topics while being interviewed for the documentary, *The Scourging of Christ*, which we'd watched in class the week before. The movie was a really bad movie, let me tell you, and I didn't want to show it, but apparently it was written into the founding charter of the school that every boy had to see the thing, or at least that's the impression I got from the theology chair. Anyway, the documentary was basically a snuff film with talking heads. Patricia O'Neil, though she obviously knew a lot about physiology, seemed to take a rather sadomasochistic pleasure in her commentary. She said things like, "The skin was literally *ripped* from his back!" and "His lungs *burned* for want of air!" Most everybody remembered her humdinger "symphony of pain" line, but me, I couldn't ignore the fact that the camera never panned below her waist, ie. what exactly were those hands up to?

"Right," I said to Max Honnold, "but let's not forget the distinction Vincent was working on earlier. Was the passion of Christ an experience of *pain* or an experience of *suffering*?"

Crickets. Maybe this was too much to expect from high school boys. I checked the clock on the TV to see how much time I had to work with. Only four minutes.

"Okay, let's say you get punched in the face..."

Vincent Stefano looked up at me with his black eye. Jesus, why the hell did I pick that as my hypothetical?

"...or kicked in the groin, or shot, or stabbed, or even crucified. Now obviously all those things would cause pain, right? But could we also say they cause suffering? Or is that going too far? Do we first need to consider the context of the situation? If so, which parts?"

More crickets. Good teachers are sometimes comfortable with silences, or so I'd been told. The clock on the TV turned to 8:47.

Tanner Baxter, who hadn't offered a goddamn relevant comment all period and could probably just sense my desperation, raised his hand.

"Yes, Mr. Baxter?"

"To answer your punch-to-the-face hypothetical..." (Adjacent Cole Prescott giggled like a naughty school girl.) "...I think sometimes it's suffering and sometimes it's pain. It's like what Vinnie said about what's the point. If somebody up and coldcocks you, okay, there was no reason for that. But other times..." And when he said this, it was like he was saying it directly to Stefano. "...other times, you get punched in the face because you need to be taught a lesson. So there's a point in that case."

Vincent said not a word. He didn't even flinch. His eyes were back on his Bible and his notebook, and the look on his face was such that I completely lost my train of thought, meaning that the last three minutes of class not only failed to climax into the awesome, goosebump-inducing conclusion I'd hoped for, but were actually kind of a clusterfuck. When the bell rang, everyone bolted, and I barely had time to yell, "Read chapter seven for tomorrow."

"I believe we're on chapter nine," said Max Honnold.

"Huh? Oh, whatever. Hey, Vinnie, hold back a minute, will you?"

We allowed time for the others to clear out. Then, when it was just the two of us, I said, "That's quite a shiner you've got there."

He didn't look away, but he didn't say anything either. Just outside the door, the hallway was suddenly very noisy, but the classroom, which was empty second period, remained quiet.

"You want to tell me how you got it?"

"No offense, Mr. Murphy, but I'd rather not. Snitches and stiches, you know."

"Yeah, okay." I gave him a looking over. He wasn't in too bad of shape aside from the black eye. No bruises on his forearms or anything. No cuts. The fight probably hadn't been much of a fight. One solid punch and he was down, poor kid. "You know, Vinnie, I thought you were smarter than this. If you were going to throw hands, why the hell did you pick someone like Tanner Baxter? Don't you know you have to fight smaller, weaker boys, preferably the unpopular ones?"

A slight grin flashed across his face. "I thought you were a pacifist, Mr. Murphy."

"What the hell gave you that impression?"

"Didn't you used to be a..." He stopped himself. "Never mind. It doesn't matter. The smaller, weaker boys aren't going out with Mackenzie Richards."

"Mackenzie Richards, huh? It's always a dame, isn't it?"

"What?"

"Vinnie, sit down a second. I feel like we should have a conversation."

He gave me a look of grave reluctance. "Don't you have to teach?"

"I don't think so. I'm usually off second period. We aren't on some kind of special schedule today, are we?"

"No, but I have to get to Calculus."

"Calculus. Good one."

He glanced at the door.

"Vinnie, I'm begging you, sit down. I'll write you a note or something. I don't get to have many of these precious teacher student moments, so just humor me, alright?"

The kid said fine and sat down.

I sat down, too, opposite him, on the big teacher's desk. I told him it wasn't fair, you know, life sometimes, especially when it came to creatures of the opposite sex.

"Okay."

"Listen, if this Mackenzie girl had any kind of head on her shoulders, I'm sure she'd dump Tanner Baxter in a second and go out with you instead."

"That's nice of you to say, Mr. Murphy, but Mackenzie *does* have a head on her shoulders, a very smart and pretty head, as a matter of fact, which is kind of why this whole thing is eating me up on the inside."

"Oh," I said. "I guess you have a point there."

"Anyway, I didn't really expect anything different. I know how things are. Tanner's strong and handsome and good at sports, and I'm weak and skinny and read pretentious novels. I can't blame Mackenzie for picking him."

"Okay, but that's more of a maturity issue."

His face brightened. "Do things really get different when people get older?"

"Is that what your parents tell you?"

He shrugged. Not even someone like Vincent Stefano was eager to admit that maybe Mom and Dad actually had some decent life wisdom to offer. Regardless, they were way off on this point, and I told him so.

"People never stop caring about looks, Vinnie, but the good news is that when you get older, most everybody gets fat or bald or just sort of run-down looking, so the ugliness spreads out in a way, and there's a more level playing field, and then suddenly personality has a chance to matter."

"That's not exactly—"

"And you know who has personality?"

He stared, dumbfounded.

"It's not people like Tanner Baxter. That kid's about as interesting as a lacrosse stick."

"Mr. Murphy, I—"

"It's people like you. And me, too, frankly. Those who've gone through the shitter and come out the other side with the scars to prove it. Look, I know it sucks right now that girls like Mackenzie Richards don't give you the time of day, but just think of all the good this'll do you in the long run."

He gave me a look like, "No offense, Mr. Murphy, but I don't see any good coming from this."

I told him okay, he was right to be skeptical. "Let me give you an honest piece of theological opinion, though. Suffering *is* a form of change. It changes you from a boring person into an interesting person, and I don't mean this glibly, but the way I see it, since we're only here for a limited amount of time, we have a moral responsibility to not be boring. That's just my opinion. You can take it or leave it."

Vincent thought a moment in the secluded quiet of second period. Then he stood up and collected his books and asked for that note excusing him from the first five minutes of Calculus.

"You know, Mr. Murphy, you're not like any of my other teachers. Don't get me wrong, in a lot of ways, you're kind of bad at your job. I'm glad you're only teaching Theology, and not a class most colleges care about."

"Mr. Stefano, please, I'm blushing."

"But we talk about important things," he said. "Really important things."

38

Not long after my conversation with Vinnie, I was pouring myself a cup of coffee in the faculty lounge when Zoey Foster, as was her habit, entered the room bearing a bottle of hazelnut creamer.

"You look happy this morning, Leo. What happened? Good class?"

"Not exactly, but I did receive a compliment afterwards. Vincent Stefano said we, quote, talk about important things. My heart is practically aflutter."

Zoey smiled and said she really liked Vincent. "He's so sweet and sensitive and a very deep thinker, too."

Unspoken: "I hope he doesn't masturbate to me like all the other boys do."

Zoey Foster was the youngest and by far prettiest female employee at Francis Xavier. She was maybe twenty-eight or twenty-nine years old, had wavy red hair, thin shoulders, small but perky breasts, a reasonable ass, and a wardrobe consisting of professional yet stylish skirt and blouse combinations. Out in the real world, where there were, you know, other women to look at, she might've registered a hard six-and-a-half, maybe a soft seven. Inside the halls of Francis Xavier, she was practically a goddess.

"Hazelnut?"

"Thank you, my dear."

I added a splash of the good stuff to my coffee and gave it a quick stir. The creamer was kind of our thing ever since the day about two months ago when I was offhandedly bitching and happened to mention that the coffee in the faculty lounge was gummy, motor-oil shit that simply could not be ingested black. To make matters worse, I informed Zoey, there were no free sugar packets, just a bunch of off-brand sweeteners that were clumpy and probably cancer-inducing.

"Oh no," she'd responded with mock concern. "I'll drop everything and get right on that."

The next morning, she arrived with my creamer, as she did every morning after that, Monday through Friday, without fail. Though there was no good reason why the bottle couldn't just live in the faculty lounge refrigerator (thus saving her the trip), I didn't have the heart to bring this up. For one thing, I enjoyed our daily conversations second period. For another, Zoey Foster, inexplicably, had a bit of a crush on me. In the past month alone, she'd brought up three different movies she'd love to go see, not to mention the fact that, totally just FYI, she really enjoyed trying out new coffeehouses on the weekend. I felt that denying her daily creamer might be letting her down too hard.

"Thanks again." I said.

"Oh, sure, don't mention it."

I noticed that Zoey was looking down at the bottle of creamer where a picture of heart-shaped steam was rising up from a cup of coffee.

"Leo," she said, arms stiff, voice trembling, "I hope you don't think this is too bold of me—"

"You never told me about your date," I interrupted.

"Huh?"

"Last Friday, remember? The blind date. You said your roommate set you up with a music critic."

"Oh, right. The music critic."

224

"How was it?" I asked, gracefully moving across the room under the pretense of picking up a JUG form from the" Important Teacher Files" table. Really, I just wanted to put some space between me and Zoey.

"Well, he wasn't so much a music critic as a guy with a blog who sometimes writes about music."

"Okay, but he likes music at least."

"I guess."

"So that's something you have in common."

"Tanner Baxter," I wrote in the top corner of the JUG form. Under "Reason(s) for Referral," I put "Doucheyness," and under "Recommended Punishment," I put "Beheading."

"I don't think I'm going to see him again," said Zoey.

"Oh? Why not?"

"I don't know. We just didn't click. These guys I keep going out with—douchiness is spelled with an 'i' by the way—they're decent and good-looking, and they've got okay jobs, you know, but they're just so...so...ugh! So boring!"

She leaned over the "Important Teacher Files" table opposite me, chin resting in her hands, giving me a look that someone more inclined might've termed "exasperated cute." Don't get me wrong. I didn't have anything against Zoey Foster personally. In fact, I rather liked the woman. She was my best friend at Francis Xavier, and actually, she was kind of my best friend in all New York. Under less complicated circumstances, we might've been more than friends, although she was twenty years my junior and inter-faculty relationships were frowned upon. The thing is, though, there was still Charley to think about. Once or twice every week for the past few months, we'd been meeting at neutral-groundy-type places like bookstores and coffee shops under the pretense that Leah deserved to know her father growing up. These meetings had been tense at first. Imagine a job interview in which the person conducting the interview doesn't believe you're at all qualified to hold the position, and you also stole a large amount of money from the interviewer, and maybe also had a role in killing the interviewer's husband. Gradually, however, the tension eased somewhat. Charley's wild success had made her more generous than before, and when she saw me with our daughter—Leah really was a beautiful little girl—I think some part of her actually believed, at least for a second, that I might not be a complete scoundrel after all.

"That's too bad about your date," I said to Zoey. "In my opinion we have a moral responsibility to not be boring."

"I couldn't agree more."

"That French Vanilla?" said Billy Thompson, the varsity baseball coach, barging into the room as if with no other intention than to disrupt our conversation.

"Oh...umm..."

"Hazelnut. Shit, I guess it'll have to do." Without asking, he took the bottle from Ms. Foster and just about filled his mug. At this point he was drinking coffee-flavored cream, not that he needed it, the fat fuck. "Tanner Baxter, huh?" He tapped his finger on the sheet where I'd written the boy's name. "Kid's got a younger brother. Seventh grader, I think. Spencer. Royce. Something like that. I hear he's six foot three and can hit mid-eighties on the gun."

Billy Thompson slurped his coffee and daydreamed about his precious, flame-throwing pituitary case. Meanwhile, I told Zoey thanks again for the creamer, but that I had better get going. There were some copies I needed to run off before third period. It broke my heart to see her face just then, but since Coach Thompson was in the room, she couldn't say anything except, "Okay, Leo. Same time tomorrow?"

I told her yes, of course, I couldn't imagine it any other way. Then I balled up Tanner Baxter's JUG form and tossed it into the recycling bin as I left.

39

Cole Prescott's final essay of the semester was on the topic of faith and prayer in daily life. It began:

Merriam-Webster defines faith as "1. Belief and trust in God. 2. Belief in the traditional doctrines of religion. 3. Firm belief in something for which there is no proof." As you can see, faith is not something that can be proven scientifically. Prayer is another thing that cannot be proven scientifically. Because both faith and prayer are things that cannot be proven, that means they are things that must be taken on faith. Put another way, it is not rational to believe in faith and prayer, which brings me to my first point. Smart people do not pray.

This is a controversial statement, especially because I am a student at Francis Xavier, a Catholic religious school. But first, what is a smart person? What does a smart person do? These are some natural questions you might ask. Let me tell you. A smart person is a man or woman who makes wise decisions. An example of a wise decision is saving money. Now that you know what a smart person is, I will show you why smart people do not pray.

Casting aside the essay, which shockingly didn't turn any more insightful in pages 2-5, I went to the kitchen to grab a beer. I'd been grading mind-numbing reflections like this all afternoon, so it was a relief to have something crisp, cold, and invigorating enter the body. I took three large gulps in quick succession, then another one, then one more just for good measure. Upon returning to the living room, I set the now two-thirds empty bottle down on the coffee table next to the stack of papers and my laptop, which was open to Francis Xavier's online gradebook.

"C-" I typed in the little box at the intersection of "Cole Prescott" and "Exam Paper."

Instantly, the computer spat out an "83" under the column "Final Grade."

"Hm," I said.

Charley looked up from her grandmother's typewriter—she was sitting on the other end of the couch—and asked what was wrong.

"It's nothing," I told her. "It's just this kid I despise somehow managed to eke out a B for the semester despite being intolerable and learning practically nothing."

"Oh," she said, looking down again.

Charley made no effort to conceal her grin as she hammered out a few more words before pushing the return lever from left to right at the margin bell.

Bing! Shunk! Chunk!

"You're going to wake Leah."

"Leah's fine. She's used to it. My writing is her favorite lullaby. See for yourself."

I got up and stood over the crib, only recently assembled. Sure enough, our daughter was fast asleep. She lay in her green onesie, open-mouthed and limp, arms extended over her head as if signaling a touchdown in some dreamland football game. It'd been almost two months now since we'd met, but still every time I looked at her, I was touched in that deep recess of my heart that understood phrases like flesh of my flesh, blood of my blood.

"What was it about?" said Charley.

"Huh?"

"The essay. From that kid you hate."

"Oh, right."

I returned to the couch, taking the middle section instead of the far cushion where I'd been sitting most of the afternoon. Charley registered this advance by glancing at the approximately six inches separating her right thigh from my left thigh. She didn't move away, as I'd somewhat feared she would, but she didn't come any closer either. The typewriter on her lap was a kind of shield, keeping her safe. Or was it an anchor, keeping her rooted? Either way, the machine held a single page from her unfinished new script, *The Fabulous Foibles of Fr. Fitzpatrick, Part II*. Everyone who was anyone was dying to see it. Would Fitz and Helena eventually reconcile? Would Elektra grow into the strong young woman we all hoped she'd become? These were questions for which I had a vested, not-entirely-theatrical interest since Charley and I had decided to table all romantic discussion for the time being and instead focus on becoming the best co-parents Leah could ask for. Not that I still didn't hold out hope, of course. How could I not hope what with a living, breathing, drooling miracle sleeping in a crib just a few feet away?

"Well?" said Charley.

I blinked.

"Are you going to tell me about the essay, or is there some kind of student-teacher confidentiality thing that forbids such discussion?"

"Oh. Sorry. It was about prayer. Specifically, how it's a waste of time."

She smiled.

"What?"

"Nothing. I just thought you would've liked a paper like that."

"Because I'm a heretic?"

"No, Leo. Because you're you."

I gave Charley a looking-over while she returned to her script. There'd been more than a few moments like this in the past two months, I mean these odd, seemingly charged but also totally offhand exchanges in which I wasn't sure whether she was growing to love me again or what. And naturally I didn't want to jinx things by requesting clarification. Part of me worried that if I moved too quickly or made too much noise, I might just spook her, and then where would we be?

The next essay on the pile belonged to Max Honnold who had also written on the topic of faith and prayer in daily life. Judging by the opening sentences, Max took a more earnest approach to his spirituality than did Cole Prescott. Nevertheless, I couldn't get more than a few paragraphs in before setting the paper aside.

"What?" said Charley, looking up again.

"I do pray," I said.

"Sorry?"

"I do pray. I mean *recently*, I've been praying."

"Leo, I didn't mean to offend—"

"No, it's okay," I told her. "You were right to think that I didn't because for a long time I didn't, but then I started again, and now I try to do it every day."

Now Charley was the one giving me a looking-over. After about ten seconds, she set her grandmother's typewriter down on the floor next to the couch and said, "Alright, when did you start?"

"I don't know. Less than a year ago. It was around the same time I started teaching."

"So the kids got to you."

"I guess you could say that."

"And what do you pray for?" said Charley.

I told her it wasn't like that. The praying I did wasn't "for" anything.

"So you just sit there and say the rosary a hundred times?"

"No, of course not. It's just...well, the method I use...you see, the tradition goes back a long way, but it's not really the first thing you think of when someone says prayer."

Charley raised her eyebrows at me. I couldn't blame her for being curious, but opening up about my spiritual life was an intimacy I hadn't anticipated for the afternoon. Not that I didn't mind the intimacy exactly. It's just I'd thought (and hoped) it would manifest itself via, you know, more conventional means.

"Well?" said Charley.

I told her it was called Ignatian Contemplation.

"Sounds fancy."

"It isn't really."

"Tell me about it."

"You actually want to know?"

"Of course."

"Why?"

"What do you mean, why? You obviously thought it important enough to tell me that you pray, so you might as well tell me how you pray, too."

Just then there came a rustling from the crib, followed by the soft cooing sound of Leah emerging from her nap. I went over to check on her and found that she was stretching her tiny arms and kicking her tiny feet.

"It's imaginative," I said. "That's the main thing. Ignatius...well, I should back up. Ignatius was the founder of the Jesuits, you know, but before he became a priest, he was this playboy soldier who spent all his free time either sleeping with women or reading chivalric novels. Then he got hit with a cannonball at some battle. I'm a little fuzzy on the details. One thing I do remember, though, is that while he was recovering from his injury, the only things he had to read were these books about Jesus and the lives of the saints. At first, Ignatius thought he was going to die of boredom, but then a funny thing happened. Once he started reading, he became enthralled. I won't go into the whole story. It's your typical one-eighty conversion kind of thing. But here's the interesting part: the type of prayer Ignatius developed, it operates on the same principles as those trashy romances he used to read. He figured out that we don't just relate to God through our thoughts and feelings. We also use our imagination."

I turned around to explain the process. First, I said, I would select a passage from scripture. A scene worked best. There needed to be people, drama, a setting. I would read the passage a few times over, and then I would close my eyes and try to imagine it. And I mean *really* try. Like I wouldn't just visualize the scene and call it good. Instead, I'd aim to get all five senses firing. Like for example, let's say I was standing next to Jesus while he smeared the mud on the blind man's eyes. In this situation, I would ask myself, what does that mud smell like right now? If I were to scoop some up and hold it in my hands, how would it feel? What kind of sound does it make between my fingers?

"So you insert yourself," said Charley.

"In a way."

"And are you always on the periphery, or do you sometimes become like a main character? And do you ever talk or ask questions? I'm not making fun. I'm just trying to get a sense of how this all works."

I told her it was different each time.

She asked, "How do you know you're actually praying and not just making things up?"

I shrugged.

"Interesting. Very interesting." Charley stood up from the couch and went into the other room. Before I could ask what she was doing, she returned with the Bible I kept at my bedside. "Let's try it."

"What? Contemplation? Right now?"

"Why not? This is all we need, isn't it? I mean, besides our thinking caps." She rested the Bible on the railing of Leah's crib and thumbed through first the Old and then the New Testament. The pages made a soft feathery sound as they flew by. Her eyes darted back and forth, scanning for a relevant passage. "You said a scene with setting and characters. Something we can really sink our teeth into."

"Yeah, a scene works best."

"Revelation would be pretty trippy, huh? Let's not do that. I'm not really in an LSD kind of mood." She turned back to the very beginning and ran through Genesis again. A few pages in, she stopped. "Here. How about this one? The story of Noah."

I nodded and said it could work.

"So we read it first?"

"Uh-huh."

"You do it, Leo. You've got more lector experience."

She slid over the Bible, and our hands touched briefly when I took it from her.

"Right. Well, okay. You want to close your eyes? Good. So this is the part right after the flood. Remember, all five senses. Put yourself into the scene." I cleared my throat and began to read. "At the end of forty days, Noah opened the hatch he had made in the ark, and he sent out a raven to see if the waters had lessened on the earth. It flew back and forth until the waters had dried out on the earth. Then he sent a dove to see if the waters had lessened on the earth. But the dove could find no place to alight and perch, and it returned to him in the ark, for there was water all over the earth. Putting out his hand, he caught the dove and drew it back to him inside the ark. He waited seven days more and again sent the dove out from the ark. In the evening, the dove came back to him, and there in its bill was a plucked-off olive leaf. So Noah knew that the waters had lessened on the earth. He waited still another seven days and then released the dove once more, and this time it did not come back."

When I'd finished the passage, I closed the Bible and set it down in the crib beside Leah. My daughter was staring up at me, curious and quiet. I wondered if she knew via a kind of fuzzy baby intuition that something sacred had just been read. I closed my eyes and tried to imagine the scene, but it was difficult, given Charley's proximity, for me to remove myself mentally. I could hear her breathing just beside me and sense her subtle movements as she shifted her weight from foot to foot. This is what extended absence from a beloved will do to a person: make you respect the physical in a way most of us take for granted.

"I'm nervous," said Charley, "and excited. The air is stale and dark and smells of so many animals. All my muscles are stiff. My skin is oily because I haven't bathed in weeks. The whole inside of this ship sounds like…well, I can hear the animals clearly in a way I couldn't before. It was because of the rain, you know, like driving on the highway for a long, long time, but now that we've pulled off, there's just this silence in the space that's such a relief."

I cracked an eye to look at her. Charley's own eyes were still closed, and she was holding onto the railing of the crib very tightly.

"I see Noah," she continued. "He's old, *very* old. The storm has been hard on his body. His arms are so frail and skinny he can't lift the hatch. I go over and help him with it, and we push up together, and when it opens…my God, Leo, it's like being born all over again. So bright. Painfully bright. And the air…the air is fresh and clean and wet. We stand there a minute, just breathing, shielding our eyes. I'm the first to go out."

I closed my eyes again and listened while Charley spoke. Soon I found myself transported. I was standing there on the deck of the ark, under the newly-emerged sun, before the endless sea, beside her.

"Do you feel the breeze?" she said. "I've never been more thankful for the wind."

"I can feel it," I said.

"It smells like salt."

"And that odor after a hard rain."

"I'm looking out over the waters now," said Charley. "The waves stretch on and on."

"All the way to the horizon."

"*Every* horizon."

"Are you afraid?" I asked her.

"Of course," said Charley. "I've never been more afraid."

"Why? Because of the water?"

"Not just the water," she said. "The whole world. It's so different now. What is this place we've sailed to?"

"Is it better, though? I mean, better than what was before?"

"I don't know. It's too early to say."

She took a deep breath, and after that, I felt her hand move over my hand and rest there, and then I felt her fingers squeeze around the top of my hand, holding it tight.

"He's taking out the bird. Do you see it, Leo? It's so eager to stretch its wings. The feathers make a nice flapping sound."

"I hear them," I said.

"It's taking off," said Charley. "It's circling high above us."

"I see it," I told her.

"And there it goes, our hope-burdened envoy, flying for the horizon."

Made in the USA
Lexington, KY
27 December 2016